A Sense of the Infinite

Also by Hilary T. Smith
Wild Awake

A Sense of the Infinite

HILARY T. SMITH

KATHERINE TEGEN BOOKS
An Imprint of HarperCollins Publishers

Katherine Tegen Books is an imprint of HarperCollins Publishers.

A Sense of the Infinite
Copyright © 2015 by Hilary T. Smith
All rights reserved. Printed in the United States of America.
No part of this book may be used or reproduced in any manner whatsoever without written permission except in the case of brief quotations embodied in critical
articles and reviews. For information address HarperCollins Children's Books, a
division of HarperCollins Publishers, 195 Broadway, New York, NY 10007.
www.epicreads.com

Library of Congress Control Number: 2014952736
ISBN 978-0-06-218471-9

Typography by Katie Fitch
15 16 17 18 19 PC/RRDH 10 9 8 7 6 5 4 3 2 1

First Edition

For A.

1

ON THE FIRST DAY OF NOE, the raspberries are always ripe. The sprinkler makes a gentle *phut-phut-phut* in the backyard, spraying misty rainbows over the grass. When I hear Noe's footsteps on the gravel, I get up from the computer and rush down the stairs. I catch the first glimpse of her out the window: Noe striding up the driveway, feet wedged into flimsy sandals, a neon-pink Band-Aid on her knee, a flossy bracelet, or several, piling up on her wrists like offerings on a shrine. I burst through the door, her name rushing out of my mouth. We collide in a spinning hug, and for those seconds we become a dervish twirling as one body on the gravel.

"Annabeth!" she sings.

"Noe!" I squeal.

And we hurry down the street without breaking contact for a second, as if our bodies have as much to say to each other as we do. We walk, and she tells me about her summer teaching back flips to the ponytailed nine-year-olds of Camp Qualla Hoo Hoo, the counselor intrigues and minor maimings. We cut across the soccer field, and I tell her about my summer scooping ice cream at the Botanical Gardens—the lady off the tour bus who got trapped in a bathroom stall, the boy who got a beesting on his tongue and almost died. We thread our way through the crowded school parking lot and trade rumors about the upcoming year, whether it was true that Mr. Harrison and Ms. Bean were getting married, if they were really putting a frozen-yogurt machine in the cafeteria.

We sit on the bleachers and pull out Noe's phone to watch the circus videos she wants to show me and listen to the music she's planning to use for her latest gymnastics routine.

We talk about all the things we're going to do when we're eighteen: save up and travel to Paris, get matching dandelion tattoos, open a restaurant where the food is sold by the ounce and eaten with tiny silver spoons.

Her friendship was a jewel I guarded like a dragon, keeping it always in the crook of my hand.

I didn't know who I would be without the shape of it pressing into my palm, without its cool glitter to light my way.

It was the first day of senior year, and Noe was striding up my driveway.

"Noe!" I called.

"Annabeth!" she screamed.

My outstretched arms found hers, and I was home.

2

MY SCHOOL, E. O. JAMES, SAT at an intersection across from a Burger King, an EasyCuts hair salon, and a funeral parlor. There was a girl in my grade whose parents owned the funeral parlor; every year on Career Day, her dad gave the same jokey speech about the perks of being a mortician. I wasn't sure why they kept bringing him back. By the time we'd graduated college and were ready to consider such career paths, technology would have advanced such that most people would probably be turned into nanopellets and shot into outer space.

The first day of school wasn't really school, more like a cut-rate carnival that got more exhausting and pointless every year.

In the morning, they made us play team-building games on the soccer fields. The team-building games largely consisted of throwing basketballs at people you despised. Occasionally, you were also supposed to capture a flag or form a human pyramid; I never figured out when or why.

After the team-building games, there was an all-school barbecue where teachers who would stare past you with glazed eyes for the rest of the year smiled and handed you an Oscar Mayer wiener instead.

After the barbecue, there was a motivational speaker, who was invariably a not-quite-famous cyclist who lost a leg to cancer and discovered the true meaning of determination.

The motivational speaker was supposed to get us excited about life, but I always ended up lost in daydreams about having cancer and dying and not having to be myself anymore. Noe loved the motivational speakers and always lined up to get their autograph, and I would hang behind her, lost in fantasy, imagining the cancer spreading through me, which would be so much better than having to clock another seventy years as Annabeth Schultz, Deeply Flawed and Reluctant Human.

It was weird to know that this first day was going to be our last one ever. When Noe and I got to school, the Senior Leaders had set up tables where you were supposed to pick up your name tag and get assigned to a team. They were wearing bright purple T-shirts with *E. O. James* on the front. The whole point of Senior Leaders was to make the school a friendlier place, but despite their best intentions they ended up terrorizing as many kids as they helped. If you got confused and didn't go where they pointed, they shouted and blew their whistles in a way that could give you a lifelong case of PTSD.

Noe wasn't afraid of the Senior Leaders.

"Come on," she said.

She grabbed my arm and we slipped around a barricade of folding tables and into the quiet cool of the school building. We hurried down the echoey hallway, two thieves in the forbidden fortress.

"Where are we going?" I said, my heart fluttering with the ecstasy of minor mischief.

"Nurse's office," said Noe.

"Don't tell me you're going to play the heatstroke card," I said. "The games haven't even started yet, she'll never believe you."

Noe hated being outdoors. I spent as much time in the forest as I could. In the fairy tale of our lives, she would be Rapunzel and I'd be Robin Hood: Noe in her tower, courted by princes, me ranging through the woods with my bow. That she managed to spend entire summers at Camp Qualla Hoo Hoo without getting so much as a sandal tan was an achievement that continued to astound me year after year.

"It's not for me," said Noe. "You need to get your health form signed for gymnastics. It's official business. I'm simply escorting you."

"That might work better as an excuse if we were actually walking in the *direction* of the nurse's office," I said.

"Details, details," said Noe. "Come on, I want to show you a few things on the beam."

We came to the gym—where I had known Noe was heading all along—and she compelled the door open with one thrust of her strong, slightly hairy arms. As we entered the empty gym I felt a pleasant shiver, remembering the afternoon last spring when Noe had taken me to talk to the gymnastics coach, Ms. Bomtrauer.

"Annabeth would like to sign up for next year's team," Noe had said, thrusting me forward like a hundred-dollar pair of shoes she had snatched out of the ten-cent box at a garage sale. "She's strong as a horse, she has a stellar physique, and she is going to be phenomenal."

I am not a leotard person, or a bathing-suit person, or really a single-layer-of-clothing person at all. I like to stay well insulated at all times, in case there is an emergency that requires me to be cold: freak snowstorm, locked in the deep freeze, battle with the Abominable Snowman. But standing in the gym, with Noe's arm around my shoulder, I found myself nodding and grinning and trying not to bounce, like a turtle so intoxicated by a songbird's tales of flight that it forgets it doesn't have wings.

Now Noe dragged the balance beam away from the wall.

"Up you go!" she commanded.

"It's too high. I need a helmet."

"Up up up!"

I mounted the beam clumsily. "What now?" I said.

Noe climbed onto the beam and began to demonstrate some easy moves. I mirrored her as best I could, holding my arms up high and trying not to wobble. I lost my balance a couple of times and had to jump off, but soon I discovered that as long as I focused my eyes on Noe and never looked down, I could stay pretty stable. Noe began to talk.

"So Leigh had a sleepover for all the girls on her soccer team, and her parents ordered all this pizza and Chinese food and they only finished half of it, and in the morning the last two pizzas, twelve fortune cookies, three orders of chow mein, and all the fried rice were gone."

"What happened to it?" I said, delighted, as always, to receive Noe's latest report on the lives of our classmates. Although I would never admit it, there was a small, proud part of my heart that believed Noe only bothered being friends with other girls so she would have stories to cackle over with me.

"Megan Bronner ate it," said Noe.

"How is that even possible? She's tiny."

"She puked it all up."

"Nooooo . . ."

"Yup. Every last bit. Leigh found a fortune floating in the toilet."

"What did it say?"

Noe twirled on her toes. "God, Annabeth, she didn't fish it out and *read* it."

"I would have read it. Now we'll never know what it said."

"Great fortune will come on the day you stop barfing. Lucky number 7, 12, 44, 72."

"Good thing she doesn't work at the ice-cream shop," I said. "They'd have to lock up the waffle cones."

Noe looked me up and down. "Now try lifting your leg," she said.

"Like this?"

"Yup. Yup. Good. Amazing. Now stop! Hold it!"

"I can't hold it!"

"Yes you can!"

The morning could have gone on like that forever: Noe and I high up on the beam, our laughter echoing through the empty gym, while the rest of the school played tedious games outside. Our best moments were always like this, I thought to myself: separate, secret, quietly superior. As I lowered my leg and attempted a half turn, I could feel senior year stretching out ahead of us in a glittering ribbon.

"Did you hear about the guy who was stalking Phinnea?" I

started to say, when the gym door creaked open and Ms. Bomtrauer's voice barked, "Ladies, what are we doing indoors?"

Thanks to Noe's unsinkable talent when it came to charming teachers, we left the gym with no more than a stern scolding for using the equipment unsupervised, plus some embarrassing cooing over my unbounded potential as a gymnast. ("You should have seen her, Ms. Bomtrauer, she did a perfect arabesque on her first try!") As we hurried to the nurse's office, I imagined myself as the girl Noe seemed to think I could be: a graceful Annabeth, ambitious and disciplined, a pony-tailed swan under bright lights. A nice girl, unimpeachable, a girl anyone would like.

For a moment the fantasy intoxicated me. I saw myself on the uneven bars, beloved, adored.

"Are you excited?" Noe said.

I said nothing, but a sheepish grin weaseled its way out from my lips.

"I knew it!" said Noe, slapping her thigh. "You are going to be incredible."

Noe was the kind of friend who could make you believe, however fleetingly, in the possibility of *incredible*. I clutched her arm close and took a deep breath of her, grateful for the thousandth time that she was mine.

THE NURSE WORE ONE OF THOSE big, shapeless nurse shirts and flowered pants, and she had gold hoop earrings. The room was a little too warm and the walls were cluttered with faded posters. I sat on the firm, high examination bench and read the slogans: DARE TO BE DRUG-FREE. EAT THE RAINBOW.

The nurse winked at me. "I'll try to make this quick so you don't miss the barbecue."

"That's okay," I said. "I don't eat meat anyway."

"Oh yeah?" said the nurse approvingly. "My younger daughter's vegetarian." She strapped the blood-pressure thing to my arm and pumped it a few times. "We call my daughter the rabbit," she said. "My husband likes to cook big steaks." She laughed a big, steak-y laugh and ripped off the Velcro armband. "Blood pressure's good. Now I need you to hop onto the scale."

I went to the creaky scale, climbed on, and stood perfectly still while she adjusted the metal tabs. There was a water balloon fight going on outside the window. Every year, Principal Beek broke out a bright orange Super Soaker and pretended to be a fun guy for five minutes.

"I'm going to zip through a few questions," said the nurse, "and we're done."

"Okay," I said.

"Any allergies?" said the nurse.

"No."

"Asthma?"

"No."

"Any medications?"

"I'm taking the Pill for acne," I said.

She gaped at me in mock disbelief. "But your skin is perfect."

"You should have seen me last year," I said. "It wasn't pretty."

I smiled, remembering the conversation I'd had with Noe on the day I got the pills.

"Ohmigod," Noe had said, snatching the packet off my desk. "Vanessa Guittard was taking these and she grew a moustache."

"What?" I'd said.

"It works the same if you take half. The every-day thing is just for people who are too dumb to remember."

Thanks to Noe's tip, I now had no zits and no moustache, and I hadn't gained a hundred pounds either, like another girl Noe knew.

"Any other meds?" said the nurse.

"Nope."

"All right."

She scribbled a note on my chart, then picked up my Clearance for Participation in Extracurricular Athletics form, signed her name, and wrote something on the bottom.

"All done?" I said.

"Almost. Which period do you have free on Thursdays?" She took a day planner out of the pocket of her shirt and paged through it.

"Second," I said. "Why?"

"Our school just got funding for a nutritionist to come in once a week. His name is Bob and he's wonderful. I'm sending all the vegetarians to talk to him. I'm putting you down for next Thursday, ten a.m." She said it with the gleefulness of a child who has just learned a new magic trick and is eager to subject it to anyone and everyone she can.

"Vegetarian doesn't mean anorexic," I said. "They even have separate entries in the dictionary."

This was one of Noe's favorite rants. *Look it up, people! Vegetarian: person who opposes the systematic torture of animals.*

13

Anorexic: person who opposes the systematic eating of food.

The nurse winked at me. "Bob's lots of fun. He can help you come up with a plan to get more protein and iron. After all, we don't want you keeling over on the high beam."

"I get more iron than the average carnivore," I said, again quoting Noe. "Did you know that spinach has more iron than steak?"

She patted my shoulder. "That's something you can talk about with Bob. It looks beautiful out there. Enjoy the rest of your day."

AT THE BARBECUE, I MOVED DOWN the food table quickly, making myself a plate from the picked-over piles of buns, cheese, chips, and watermelon. I fished a can of soda out of the ice-filled garbage can and walked over to where Noe and Steven were sprawled under a tree.

"Hey, doll," said Noe. "How'd it go?"

I sank into the grass with my plate.

"Oh, fabulous," I said. "I have an appointment with Bob the Nutritionist. She's sending all the vegetarians to talk to him, so watch out."

"Are you kidding me?" said Noe.

I shook my head. "Better keep your meatless ways on the sly or you'll be next."

Noe made a hiss of exasperation. "She should be sending all the carnivores to the school psychiatrist to get their heads checked for psychopathy."

Steven whimpered, midway through a bite of his hamburger. Noe picked up the top half of her bun and chucked it at his head. "That includes you, Cow Killer McNeil."

"My mommy says that hamburgers come from the Happy Farm," said Steven in a little-boy voice.

Noe shot him a dark look. "Well, Mommy lied."

Noe and Steven had been dating since June. He was typical Noe material: intelligent and well mannered, with a special talent (acting!), professional parents (lawyers!), and none of the character flaws (a fondness for hallucinogens! the playing of team sports! weakness in grammar and punctuation!) that Noe held in such contempt. I'd watched him play the part of Willy in *Death of a Salesman*, but had never interacted with him close up until Noe announced, just before exam time, that she and he were an item.

Steven had Noe's favorite hoodie in his lap and he was mending the kangaroo pocket with a needle and thread. It was jarring to see Noe's hoodie receiving surgery from a boy I still considered basically a stranger. I knew they'd talked on the phone every day over the summer, and he'd even driven up to visit her at Camp Qualla Hoo Hoo, but because this had all taken place outside my sight, my brain still had Steven filed in the "abstraction" category and had not yet updated him to a living, breathing reality. *What are you doing?* I almost said when I saw Noe's hoodie spread out on his lap. *That's mine.* Noe's boyfriends demonstrated a degree of devotion I still found incredible after more than three years of knowing her. Whether this trait was something Noe selected for or cultivated after the fact was a mystery I was still unraveling.

I cracked open my soda and took a sip.

"I didn't even know we had a nutritionist," Noe said.

"They just got funding for him. Yippee."

"They can afford a nutritionist, but they can't spring for new gym leotards?"

"The idea is to fatten everybody up to the point that we fit in the saggy old ones."

Noe made a face. "Bad mental image," she said. She picked up the rest of her bun and started throwing pieces of it at a crow that was eyeing us from the grass.

I watched the way it hopped forward to snatch them.

"Caw, caw," Steven said.

5

IT WAS WEIRD TO SEE ALL the new freshmen swarming around at the barbecue, talking and laughing as if they already owned the place.

When I started high school, I was a total mess.

After prolonged backroom deliberations, my mom and grandmother had determined that the summer before freshman year was a good time to inform me that I was half monster. My crazy cousin Ava caught wind of the plan and beat them to it.

It was Ava's birthday and I'd been charged with keeping her corralled in her room while the adults decorated the table and put the finishing touches on her cake. We sat on her bed, and she turned up the volume on the screaming music she kept playing twenty-four hours a day, her version of a white-noise machine.

"How much has your mom told you about your dad?" she'd said.

I blushed and shrugged. Ava and I used to play together when we were little, but when she started high school Ava changed. Now when we hung out, it felt like she was always pushing and pushing, trying to get a reaction. "Do you know what this is?" and she would show me a cut on her arm. Or she would name the creepiest boy at her school and tell me all the things she had done with him, or worse, say that he liked me and wanted to go out. I longed to be in the bright kitchen with Mom and Nan. I could hear them laughing, shouting at Uncle Dylan to find them some tape to wrap Ava's present.

"His name is Scott," I said. "He went to Northern. They only slept together once. He was mean to Mom and she didn't want him around me."

Mom had dropped out of college to have me. She was nineteen. I'd never met my dad, but I imagined him as the popular quarterback in a teen movie, the one who starts falling in love with the girl from the outdoors club, only to cave in to social pressure and publicly snub her in favor of the hot cheerleader. I knew lots of other kids whose parents weren't together, so my lack of a father had never caused undue torment, although it was true that Mom was the youngest parent at my school.

"She didn't sleep with him," Ava said. "He raped her. They're going to tell you before school starts. I heard them talking about it yesterday."

I dug my hands into Ava's quilt. In the kitchen, laughter, banging cupboards, the finding of candles, the taking down of plates. Ava was a fan of dark secrets and skeletons in the closet. She had subjected me to some pretty disturbing stories over my lifetime, but this one beat them all.

"Everyone was shocked when she decided to keep you," Ava said. "She came *this close* to giving you up for adoption. My dad says the whole time she was pregnant, she hardly spoke at all. She wouldn't even tell anyone what happened until almost eight months. She must have felt like there was this monster growing inside her and it was too late to stop it."

Ava was studying my face for a reaction. I kept it carefully blank, a skill I had learned from other encounters in Ava's room. *Monster*, I thought to myself, feeling the shape of the word settle into me, feeling it quietly reconfigure every cell in my body, like hitting the translate command by accident and seeing all the writing on your screen suddenly and incontrovertibly turn to Japanese.

"You don't believe me, do you," said Ava.

I shook my head.

"Or you do believe me, and you don't want to show it."

I'd kept still. There was no wriggling out of Ava's grasp once she started in on you. She preempted every escape, called you on every strategy. She was astonishingly good at reading people, which is part of what made her so terrifying: Ava always knew what you were thinking.

"You should try to find him someday," Ava had said. "I would if I were you. I'd get my friends together and go to his house and beat the shit out of him."

I swallowed hard. I'd never thrown a real punch, let alone beat anyone up.

"You should probably get tested," Ava continued. "Who knows what kind of diseases he had?"

Monster, my brain was still thinking. *Monster*.

"Are you crying?" Ava said.

I focused my eyes on the Satan poster on Ava's wall. Satan had a black goatee and piercing yellow eyes. He was ripped, too. Arnold Schwarzenegger in Hades. "No," I'd said.

Ava took my chin in her hands and looked straight into my eyes. Her irises were purple from contact lenses. It was like staring into the eyes of a sea snake.

"You're lucky," Ava said. "It takes some people a lifetime to figure out how fucked up the world is, and you got to find out at thirteen."

From the kitchen, Mom had called us. "A-*va*, Anna-*beth*, time for ca-*ake*."

Ava let go of my face. My chin hurt where her fingers had held it. "Don't tell them I told you," she said. "Promise."

"I promise," I said.

Just then, Nan opened the door. She peered into the room in her Nannish way, her pants dusted with icing sugar. The scent of cake wafted in the open door, along with the sounds of the adults in the living room.

"Ava, Annabeth, we are ready for you to come out."

"Okay, Nanna," said Ava with an angelic smile. She hopped off the bed, suddenly bouncy.

I went to the bathroom and stared into the mirror, wondering how I'd managed to go thirteen years without noticing.

6

MOM AND NAN HADN'T TOLD ME for another week.

At my friend Hailey's pool party, I'd sat on the edge in a sweater and jeans and wouldn't swim. If I got into the water, people would see my monster-body and they would know.

At lunch, I couldn't eat. If I ate, the monster would be eating, too, and if it grew any bigger it would crowd out the only part of me that was still good.

Shopping with Mom, all I could feel was the shame and horror throbbing out from me in a tortured halo. Up until that point, I'd had no filter. Now, for the first time, I grew watchful. I pulled my hands up into the sleeves of my sweatshirt and strained to hear double meanings in everything Mom said.

"What's up, Annabean?" Mom asked. "You're never this quiet."

"Just daydreaming," I said and twitched my mouth into a smile.

Finally, the night arrived. Nan came over and they cooked my favorite dinner, and instead of playing Scrabble like we normally did, they sat me down on the couch to talk, as if I were a cancer patient about to go in for a frightening surgery.

"Annabeth," said Mom, "your grandma and I need to talk to you about something that you might find pretty upsetting."

I sat very still. If I made a sound too early, they would know that I knew. So I killed the howl that was struggling to escape me, wrung its neck like a rabbit, and dropped it as far down as it would go.

"What is it?" I'd said.

My father was a boy Mom had known from some of her classes. He was friendly and a flirt, which had made things harder after the canoe trip. People take your side when it's a stranger with a knife, less so when it's a handsome boy playing "Blister in the Sun" at a campfire sing-along.

Mom said she'd always known she wanted to have a kid, and even though it happened in a terrible way, she knew she was going to love me just as much as any other baby. The way Mom told it, the story was smooth and hopeful. She didn't mention the part about not speaking for eight months, or how she'd almost given me up for adoption. Maybe she was saving that conversation for when I was an adult.

"Did he go to jail?" I'd asked.

Ava had already told me that he hadn't, but I had to ask things or they'd figure out that I already knew.

"The laws aren't very smart," said Nan. "At the time, some other women in your mom's situation were running into problems with custody. We didn't want there to be any chance that he could come along someday and say, *I want my kid.*"

I nodded. In my head, I was imagining a hairy stranger breaking through our front door and dragging me away. Maybe it would have been better if I had been adopted. At least then Mom could have finished college and started her life over, instead of ending up back in her hometown, working at No Frills, while people she'd known all her life treated her like trash.

Mom and Nan were back to talking about how special I was and how proud of me they were.

"We'll go for a hike tomorrow," said Mom, "and we can talk about it as much as you want."

I wondered if Mom was sick of our dusty little forest, and the dusty little life to which I had consigned her. On the trail, the next day, I was too conscious of my arms and legs, my eyes and hands and hair.

"Are you angry, Annabeth?" Mom had asked. "I didn't

want to tell you when you were too little to understand. But I didn't want to wait too long either, because you're growing up fast, and if, God forbid, you ever find yourself in a situation, I want you to have a better chance than I did."

I'd never seen her so uncertain. Mom had always seemed invincible to me. She could walk the farthest and carry the heaviest pack. And as horrible as it was to find out that the delinquent-but-redeemable father I'd imagined was actually a demon, to glimpse a crack in Mom's invincibility was almost as shattering.

"Why would I be mad at you?" I'd said. "You didn't do anything wrong."

I imagined Mom getting back into her canoe the morning after it happened. Why hadn't she told anyone? Why hadn't she clawed his face off?

Monster, monster, monster, said the pumping of my heart.

Monster, monster, monster, until it was as normal as the sound of my own breath.

My first day at E. O. James, I got lost in the hallways and almost had a panic attack when a senior boy named Louis Vallero startled me in the out-of-the-way stairwell where I was hiding with a book.

At the barbecue, someone handed me a hot dog and I didn't know what to do with it. I couldn't see anywhere to throw it out, and I was about to wrap it in a napkin and hide it when a girl I didn't recognize wrinkled her nose at me.

"Gross, right?" she'd said. *"Welcome to high school, have some murdered pig parts."*

"I know," I said, even though I wasn't even vegetarian at that point, just unhappy and overwhelmed.

"I'm Noe. What's your name?"

I'd hesitated. "Annabeth."

Since the summer, it had hurt me to say my own name. I wanted to go live in the forest, with sticks in my hair, like a medieval leper. At least that would be honest; at least that way, I wouldn't have to pretend to be happy and normal. Nobody expects a medieval leper to make friends.

Noe didn't seem to notice my leperhood. "Will you come to the bathroom with me?" she said. "It's kind of an emergency."

We started walking. "What happened?" I'd said.

"The Senior Leaders made me eat Skittles," Noe said. "You know they're made out of boiled horse hooves, right? I told them I was vegetarian, and they didn't care."

Her distress was palpable. We hurried into the school building and I held Noe's hair as she threw up the detested substance.

"You *understand*," Noe had said. "My best friend at my old school was all, 'Oh my God, you're bulimic,' and I'm like, 'Bulimics eat an entire chocolate cake and puke it up. I'm just trying to get this dead animal out of my body, if that's okay with you.'"

I'd felt a wave of protectiveness toward her, this vulnerable girl with oily black hair who the Senior Leaders had force-fed horse hooves. A wave of pride, too: I was not the shrill, childish friend of eighth grade. I was the one who *understood*.

I could be the friend who understood. It was better than being a monster. I had known Noe for only ten minutes, but already I could feel that protecting her would give me a purpose, give my tortured energy somewhere to go.

I had hardly spoken all day—all summer, it felt like—but walking next to Noe, words started spilling out of me. It was as if the cold hand that had sealed me off from the rest of humankind had left one airhole open, the airhole of Noe. I found to my surprise that I could breathe again, and laugh. The effect diminished when she paused to talk to teachers, and came back again when we walked on. I observed it with fascination, this loophole in my otherwise complete suffocation. I could be a normal human, as long as I was interacting with Noe.

Noe wanted to know where I lived, and which school I had gone to before E. O. James, and if I had heard that Ms. Kravenko was the hardest for math, and if I wanted to sign up for gymnastics with her because I looked like I would be good at it. She told me all about her old boyfriend, Sean, and a summer camp with a weird name where she was going to be a junior counselor the next year.

By the time we'd settled into our auditorium seats to hear the motivational speaker, I was completely devoted to her.

With Noe beside me, I never got lost in the halls anymore. I stopped worrying about Louis Vallero. I kept her always in my field of vision, a guiding star.

"You found a friend," Mom said. "That's wonderful."

I peeled the pepperoni off the pizza we were sharing and stacked it dutifully on the edge of my plate.

1

ONE OF THE HAPPYFUN ASPECTS OF the first day of
school this year was that the Senior Leaders spent the whole
day pelting people with candy.

There was candy in the halls and candy in the bathroom
sinks and candy in the cracks between the auditorium seats.
Someone threw a Tootsie Roll at the motivational speaker,
causing Mr. Beek to hand out the first suspension of the
year.

By two p.m., the school was filled with weightless wrappers
that floated around the halls like shiny ghosts.

"This is appalling," Noe said as we walked through
an entire hallway full of Reese's Pieces that made rickety

crunching sounds underfoot.

Steven crouched and scooped up a handful. Noe slapped at his hand, but he got it to his mouth and crammed the candy in.

"Some would call it delicious," he said.

WHEN I GOT HOME FROM SCHOOL, Mom was sitting at the kitchen table sorting through a pile of mail. She was still in her uniform, her brown hair pulled into a ponytail, her feet still laced into the Converse sneakers that made her look even younger than she was.

"Hey, Annabean," she called when I walked in. "Have a sandwich. I brought home a whole tray."

Mom works the checkout at No Frills. One frill of working at No Frills is employees get to take home the premade deli sandwiches at the end of the day. They come wrapped in stretchy plastic with a capital letter slashed on in permanent marker. *T* for turkey, *H* for ham, *R* for roast beef, *V* for veggie.

I didn't think the limp and mustardy sandwiches were much of a frill, but Mom loved them.

"They're meat," I said, ducking into the kitchen to inspect the shrink-wrapped array.

"Pick it out."

My mother's advice generally boils down to "Pick it out," whether you are dealing with a slice of baloney or an arrow in the heart.

I took a sandwich marked T and started to dissect it, picking out the turkey and everything that had touched it and filling the newly empty space with leftover guacamole.

"Come take a look at this," Mom said.

I wandered to the table with my modified sandwich, and she tossed me a glossy booklet from Northern University.

"Ooh," I said, and sank down into a chair across from her.

Mom had gone to Northern for one year before dropping out to have me, and she talked about it like it was the best place on earth. Some people would hate the place where a terrible thing had happened, but to her, it was a paradise interrupted. She didn't say it in so many words, but we both knew it would mean a lot to her for me to go there. That it would mean everything.

I flipped past the sections on academics and sports and went straight to the photos of the dorms. Back in June, the day before Noe left for Camp Qualla Hoo Hoo, we'd spent all afternoon browsing the IKEA website and fantasizing about our future college dorm room. We were going to get a Winkl bead curtain and a Gulört rug and a set of Buffwak bowls and cups for when we felt like eating cereal for dinner instead of going to the cafeteria. I'd loaded the Northern University website Mom and I had been looking at the night before, and we'd pored over the list of campus clubs and decided which ones to join: People for the Ethical Treatment of Animals, the Northern University Sophisticated Tea Party Society, the gymnastics team for Noe, and the Campus Outdoors Club for me. We'd get a cactus plant named Hector and a goldfish named Boris, and in our second year, we'd move off campus so we could get a cat.

"There's a bunch of stuff from E. O. James, too," said Mom. "Did you want me to write a check for the senior camping trip?"

She slid the flyer across the table. I picked it up and skimmed it. Three nights in the Tuscarora wilderness, led by Ms. Hannigan and Mr. Von Ekelthorpe. My cousin Max had gone in his senior year. They'd hiked under the moonlight and gone swimming in freezing water. One night, a bear had wandered through their campsite and started rummaging through the food they'd forgotten to put away, and Ms. Hannigan scared it off by banging on a pot and singing "Old MacDonald Had a Farm."

"I have a gym meet that weekend," I said.

"Can't you skip it?" said Mom.

I shook my head, annoyed. "It's important," I said. "You can't miss the first one."

Noe had already enlisted me to help her take photos for the yearbook and videos for the team website she was setting up. We were going to work on it at her house after the meet.

"Too bad," Mom said. "You've been looking forward to it ever since Max told you that story about the bear."

It bugged Mom when I changed my plans because of Noe. And it bugged me that she made such a big deal out of it.

"Mom," I said. "You know we only have one class together this year. It's really important to Noe for me to be there, and I'm not just going to ditch her. I don't know anyone who's going on the camping trip anyway."

Her disappointment was a fine mist that clung to my clothes all the way upstairs. I took the new leotard out of my drawer and held it for a moment, its synthetic shimmer a promise of the newer, shinier person I might finally become.

9

I BROUGHT THE NORTHERN UNIVERSITY booklet to school. In English, Noe scrutinized the Food Services page.

"The freshman cafeteria doesn't sound that great for vegetarians," she said, wrinkling her nose at the list of food options.

"It says they have a salad bar," I said helpfully.

"That can mean anything," said Noe. "Bacon bits. Tuna. Chicken."

"Hmm," I said. "Maybe we can get a mini-fridge in our room."

"Oh, here we go," said Noe. "Smoothie machine."

I breathed an inward sigh of relief. Noe had said yes to Northern as a first choice back in June, but she could be fickle at the best of times, and I knew that our college roommates plan could be thrown off by an errant bacon bit just as easily as by something important like academics.

"Ladies," called Mrs. Fessendorf. "Are we discussing *The Waste Land* and identifying three instances of allusion?"

"Yes, Mrs. Fessendorf," sang Noe.

"Good."

She moved the booklet to her lap and we continued to browse it.

"Student-run coffee shop," Noe read. "We could get jobs there. I've always wanted to be a barista."

"Ladies!"

Noe smiled at her.

"Just planning our future, ma'am," she said.

10

THE NUTRITIONIST WAS A PLUMP, pale, sad-looking thirtysomething who seemed uncomfortable in the tiny phys-ed-office-slash-storage-room, crammed behind Ms. Bomtrauer's desk with the basketballs and the kettlebells. When I showed up for my appointment, he had an audiobook playing on the beat-up CD player, a narrator with a plodding nasal voice reading a fantasy novel. *"Nay," said the serving wench, "I'll not wed thee." "I think ye shall," said Prince Everstall, drawing his blade.* The nutritionist startled and smacked the CD player's stop button just as Prince Everstall was about to nick the laces on the serving wench's bodice. He blushed and brushed at the desk, sweeping a box of Cheez-Its into the trash.

"You must be Annabeth," he said, extending a clammy hand for me to shake.

"The one and only," I said.

He was wearing a tweed jacket that was much too warm for the weather. It looked like he'd gotten lost on his way to Harvard and wandered into E. O. James by mistake.

"I'm Bob," he said. "Please, have a seat." He gestured at a cracked plastic chair wedged between a box of rugby cleats and a pile of soccer jerseys. When I sat down, it made a sound of protest and collapsed underneath me.

"Oh dear," said Bob. "Are you okay?"

I picked myself and the chair up from the floor and sat down again gingerly. My knee was throbbing where it had banged the desk.

"They're supposed to put in a better one," said Bob apologetically.

"Really?" I said. "I thought it was a test. If you break the chair, grapefruit diet. If you don't break the chair, weight-gain pellets."

Bob smiled. "That would be quite the system. There's a beautiful sort of Procrustean logic to that."

"Indeed," I said.

He looked like an academic type, I thought again. The hair, the voice, the tweed jacket. I wondered what he was doing in a basketball storage closet at E. O. James.

I braced myself in the chair. It was threatening to buckle again. "Can we get down to business?" I said. "This is kind of uncomfortable."

"Sure, sure," he said. "Let's start with a simple question-naire."

He fumbled under his desk and took out a textbook. *Applied Nutrition.*

"What's that for?" I said.

"I'm still finishing my master's degree," he said. "This is my practicum." He flipped around inside the textbook for a few seconds, checked the table of contents, and finally arrived, sweaty-fingered, at the right page.

"Am I your first subject?" I said.

He looked up. Another one of those shy, apologetic smiles flitted across his face. "Actually, yes."

Aha, I thought. *A discount nutritionist.* Good thing the nurse hadn't sent Noe to see Bob. She would have eaten him alive.

He cleared his throat. "Just so you know," he said, "every-thing you say here will be taken in complete confidence. Please be honest with your answers. Are you ready?"

I nodded, trying not to laugh.

Bob the Nutritionist read from the textbook, his eyes never leaving the page. "Do you obsess about your weight?" he said.

"No."

"Count your calories?"

"No."

"Binge and purge?"

"No."

"Abuse laxatives?"

I grimaced. "*No.*"

He ran through a dozen more questions, ticked a few boxes, and then added the columns up.

"You're not anorexic or bulimic," he said glumly, as if this was a great disappointment. I realized he must be looking forward to his first real anorexic the way new firefighters look forward to their first blaze. Seeing his face, I found myself feeling almost disappointed too. He seemed like a nice man, and I was sorry to let him down.

"I know," I said apologetically. "The only reason I'm here is because the nurse has a thing about vegetarians."

"Ah," said Bob. "I see."

He groped around his desk and drew out a slender file folder. From the folder, he located a sheet of paper, which he studied closely, going *Hmmm, hmmmm* and nodding as he read. "This note from the nurse says you *are* a few pounds underweight. Do you ever have trouble eating?"

He blinked at me from behind his goggle glasses. His face, I noticed, was broad and open, anxious to please. He looked like a plump elf. A sad elf. I wanted to open the door of the cramped office and shoo him back into the woods where he belonged.

I hesitated. "Not really," I said.

Bob looked lugubrious. I felt bad for him, in spite of myself. "When I was a kid, I went through this phase where I gnawed on sticks and stones," I volunteered.

He seemed to perk up. "Oh?"

It was true. Sometimes, when I was mad at Mom for walking too fast when we went on hikes, I'd suck on a stone so that when my father or my fairy godmother or Minnie Mouse or my fantasy-creature-of-the-moment finally showed up, they would see how mean she was—poor Annabeth, dragged all over the woods with nothing to eat but stones!—and take me away.

"But I don't do that anymore."

Bob slumped again.

"Don't look too disappointed," I said. "I'm sure you'll find plenty of anorexics if you hang out around this place long enough."

"I'm not here only for the anorexics," said Bob. "Maybe there's something else I can help you with. For this month, how about you keep a journal of everything you eat, and we'll take a look at it together and see if there's anything that could use some tweaking."

"You mean you want me to come back?"

Bob closed his textbook and slipped my nurse's record back into its file. "Yes, sure. Why don't you come back and we'll, um, we'll look at the food journal and figure out how to proceed."

"How to *proceed*?"

"Make a plan, set some goals."

He wasn't meeting my eyes. I raised my eyebrows at him. "This doesn't have anything to do with your funding, does it?" I said.

He blushed a deep tomato red. "How does late October sound to you?" he tapped a box on his calendar.

"Do I have to?"

"I can't sign off on this until I've reviewed a food journal. So yes, you do."

I got up from the broken chair and started to collect my backpack. The nutritionist pulled open the squeaky desk drawer. "I have pizza coupons," he said, brandishing a sheath of them held together by an elastic band. "If it makes it any better."

"Pizza coupons."

"One for each session."

I hesitated. Bob looked up at me imploringly, coupons in hand. I thought of what my nan always said, about never passing up an opportunity to help a person in need. The nutritionist seemed like a nice person, and he definitely had a need. I shrugged. "I guess so," I said.

I GOT TO ART A FEW minutes late and took the empty seat next to Steven. On the whiteboard at the front of the room, Mr. Lim had written *WORK PERIOD: STILL LIFE*. Beneath the whiteboard was a table with an apple and two pears. The classroom was overbright and morguelike. I took out my sketch pad and pencil case and arranged them on my part of the table. Steven turned to me.

"How was the nutritionist?" he said.

It surprised me that he remembered. "Fine," I said.

I fussed with my pencil sharpener, pretending to have exacting requirements for the pointiness of my lead. I didn't normally interact much with Noe's boyfriends. They seemed to exist on a different plane—too clean, too conspicuously *smart*. Sometimes the whole situation reminded me of a Venn diagram: there was the place where Noe and I overlapped absolutely, and two moon-shaped zones where there was no overlap at all. Noe's boys lived in the no-overlap zone, and my obsession with being outdoors—things we happily tolerated in each other, but to which we didn't pay much attention. I touched my newly sharpened pencil to the page and started in on the first pear.

Steven leaned his chin on his knuckles and watched me lazily. "Which nurse sent you?" he said.

"I don't know her name."

"Curly hair? Earrings?" He made curly hair and earrings gestures with his hands, bobbing them around his head and ears.

"Yes."

"I got her for my meningitis shot last year. She thinks everyone's either anorexic or depressed. It's, like, her thing."

"Which one are you?"

"Depressed, obviously. I'm a boy. It's like a neonatal ward in there: girls get pink, boys get blue."

"Did she make you see a counselor?" I said.

"Oh yes. I'm quite unstable. Ask me to show you my mood journal sometime."

"I'm supposed to keep a food journal."

"Can I see it?"

"I haven't eaten anything yet."

"Aha! Anorexic."

"It's only been five minutes since the appointment."

Steven reached into his pocket and pulled out a roll of Life Savers.

"Here," he said.

"They're all linty." I put one of the Life Savers in my mouth, then spat it out. "Yeck. This tastes like pocket."

"Write it down," said Steven.

I wrote it in my notebook: *linty Life Saver, 2 p.m.* Then I put my notebook aside and started in on the pear again, because surely the conversation wasn't going to last for the entire class. Steven watched me draw.

"Do I make you uncomfortable?" he said.

I looked up. "What?"

"Don't worry," he said. "I won't be offended. I'm just curious."

I reddened, not wanting to explain about the Venn diagram. "I don't know," I said. "I guess we don't really know each other outside of Noe."

"Is that what it is?" said Steven. "In that case, we must introduce ourselves. I'm Steven."

He held out his hand. I shook it. "Annabeth," I said.

"Pleased to make your official acquaintance, Annabeth. Let's be friends."

"Okay," I said. Then, because I felt guilty, I burst, "I didn't mean that we weren't already *sort* of friends. By association."

"I don't like knowing people through people," he said evenly. "It feels too much like regurgitation."

"Ah," I said. "Hmm."

I sketched in the apple and added some wavy lines to indicate brightness. Steven picked up his pencil and used it to render a photographically perfect set of fruit on his page.

At the front of the room, Mr. Lim glanced at his digital watch.

"Anybody who has not handed in their self-portrait, please do so before the end of class," he announced into the middle distance.

"Shit," I murmured.

"Did you say *shit*?" Steven said. "I was wondering whether you were a swearer."

I flipped my sketchbook page and started drawing frantically. "I forgot my self-portrait," I said. "Can you just—I need to concentrate."

I drew an oval for a face, but without a mirror I realized I had no idea what I looked like. I knew I had two eyes, a nose, a mouth, and hair, but without an image to copy from I was suddenly unsure of the dimensions. *Whatever*, I thought to myself, *I'll take the redo.* Mr. Lim was famous for his pass/redo system, which meant you could barf up a self-portrait in the last ten minutes of class with full confidence that you could do it over. Around the classroom, I noticed a few other kids whose drawing had picked up a rather mysterious speed and urgency. At least I wouldn't be the only smudgy ten-minute portraiteer.

"Are you sure you don't have body dysmorphia?" Steven said, openly inspecting the page I was trying to hide with my free hand. "This portrait strikes me as rather sumoesque."

"It's fine," I hissed. "I don't have time to start again."

"Oh, come on," said Steven. "You can do better than that. Have some standards."

I was about to tell Steven I didn't have artistic standards, but instead I grabbed my eraser and scrubbed at the page. The clock now showed four minutes remaining in class. I drew a new oval.

"Too wide," said Steven. "Your face is skinnier than that."

I flipped to a new page and drew a skinny oval.

"Skinnier," said Steven.

"Aaaargh, it doesn't matter."

"Yes it does. Do you want the nutritionist to think you see yourself as enlarged by two hundred percent?"

"He's not going to see it."

"Are you kidding me? I tailor all my art pieces for maximal psychoanalytic potential. It keeps Ricardo busy."

"I just need to—" I waved him off irritably.

"Okay," said Steven. "Here we go. Eyes go in the middle

of the face. Middle of the face. Nope, that's the crown of your skull. Are your eyes on top of your head?"

I ripped the page out of my sketchbook and crumpled it up.

"Wha—why'd you do that?" said Steven. "You were doing great."

"I can't draw under pressure," I said, flipping to a fresh sheet.

The bell started to ring.

"Shit."

Steven opened his backpack, rummaged around, and pulled out a bundle of sticks tied up with a piece of string. "Here," he said.

"What the heck is that?"

I didn't mean to bark at him, but I really wanted to get good grades that year and it pained me to lose marks on a throwaway assignment.

"Your self-portrait," said Steven.

"It has to be a drawing."

"Negatory. The assignment said 'Any Medium.'"

"Why do you have sticks in your backpack?"

"Prop from a scene we did in Drama this morning. Elsinore Forest to Dunsinane."

"You're out of your mind."

"Hand it in."

"Hey, Mr. Lim, here are some sticks."

"It's a sculpture."

The bell stopped ringing. Kids were filtering into the room for the next class.

"Trust me," said Steven. "I've been getting straight A's in art for years."

I ripped a piece of paper from my sketchbook and wrote, *RAW MATERIALS: Portrait of the Artist as a Bundle of Dry Sticks.*

"That's more like it," Steven said, nodding his approval. "Barren. Dead. Fleshless. Starving. Your nutritionist is going to trip balls."

Steven McNeil. I thought to myself, as I hurried to Mr. Lim's desk with my sticks, that he was one of the most irritating people I had ever met, and also the most confoundingly entertaining.

12

I TOLD NOE ABOUT THE NUTRITIONIST, feeling only slightly guilty as I exaggerated the details of his audiobook.

"*Suck my blade, you horny wench?*" screeched Noe. She shuddered theatrically. "Christ, what a perv. Trust good old E. O. James to hire the creepiest-possible fake nutritionist."

"I'm keeping a food journal," I said.

"What?"

"You know. So we can make a plan, set some goals, and figure out how to proceed."

"But you're not—"

"I know. He's bribing me with pizza coupons until he finds

a real anorexic to work on."

Noe smacked herself in the forehead. "Oh, Bethy," she said. "This cannot end well."

"It can end in free pizza," I said.

THAT AFTERNOON WAS THE FIRST GYMNASTICS
practice of the year. I felt a little silly being the only new senior
on the team, but with Noe to smooth things over it wasn't too
bad. During warm-up stretches, we sat in a circle with the other
senior girls, and soon she had them all laughing with my story
about Bob the Nutritionist's dirty fantasy novel. By the time
Ms. Bomtrauer had us break into levels to start training on the
beam, bars, vault, and floor, I felt like I was in. Even though
I was lumped into Level One with an assortment of earnest
freshmen, it wasn't so bad. My allegiance was clearly to Noe
and Kaylee and Rhiannon and the other seniors on the opposite side of the gym.

Walking home with Noe after practice, I was tired and elated.

The air still felt like summer: humid and warm. The gutters were littered with popsicle sticks stained pink and orange, and crushed Slurpee cups from the Avondale store.

"Want to know something crazy?" Noe said. "Steven's mom told me he attempted suicide last winter."

"What? Why?"

"He was already depressed and his stupid friend got him really drunk, which is the worst thing for depressed people. He's just lucky someone stopped when they saw him on the bridge."

"Whoa," I said. I'd never met anyone who had tried to kill himself before.

"His mom says I pretty much saved his life," Noe said. "She hasn't seen him so happy in years."

I thought of the note Noe had shown me after English, the one Steven had tucked into her copy of *Modern Western Poetry*. He'd copied out a Shakespeare quote in exquisite calligraphy: *Hear my soul speak/The very instant that I saw you did/My heart fly to your service.*

That was it, I'd thought to myself. That was it exactly.

"He does seem happy," I agreed.

We came to the intersection where we normally said goodbye. "Want to come over?" Noe said.

"Only if we can take the shortcut."

"Bethy, I'm wearing ballet slippers."

"So go barefoot."

"*You* go barefoot, Rambo."

I dragged her off the sidewalk and onto the tiny trail that led into the maples, and soon Noe was singing. The leaves were still green, still soft and whispering, like summer dresses the trees had yet to exchange for sturdier clothes. A broken bottle sparkled in the dirt.

In my head, I was doing spins on the uneven bars. I was on a plane to Paris. I was dropping a goldfish into a bowl, and I'd never been happier in my life.

SEPTEMBER IN OUR TOWN IS THE fastest month, and also the most beautiful. The blue of the sky is made sharper by the yellowing leaves, the air turns clear and pure, and the roadside fruit stands that hawk peaches and plums all summer set out baskets of apples and pears instead. Tourists still come by the busload to stand by our waterfall in disposable raincoats and buy fudge from the little gift shops that clog the main road, to ride the SkyTram back and forth across the river and pay too much for a horse-drawn carriage to clop them up and down the historical district's flower-lined streets. At school, the bulletin boards are plastered with sign-up sheets for sports and clubs and volunteer groups, and everyone seems to rush around in a great hurry before the lethargy of winter sets in.

It sucked not having most of my classes with Noe, like we'd had every other year. Normally, we did all our group projects together, but now when I met her by our lockers, she'd be bickering over animal rights with Steven or chatting about a physics assignment with Kaylee and Rhiannon or helping some lumbering Senior Leader conjugate the verb *comer*, and I wouldn't know what they were talking about. Noe had always been friendly with a wide range of people, but they'd stayed on the periphery. Now that I wasn't there to be Noe's project partner, the peripheral people were stepping in to fill the vacuum: to make inside jokes in Spanish class, to get mutually indignant over an unfair biology test, to make plans to go to the Java Bean after school.

"Lindsay's thinking we should make reservations at Luigi's," she'd say, and after some questioning it would emerge that she and Lindsay Harris had spent Biology making plans for the homecoming dance.

I did my best to keep up with the changes. I said hey to all the people Noe said hey to. In practice, I stayed with Noe's group as long as I could before being banished to the Level Ones.

I learned to point my toes when I cartwheeled and sweep my arms up when I landed. I waited in line with the other Level Ones to take my turn running at the vault or swinging on the bars. Mostly Noe was too busy working on her own routines to talk much during that part of practice, but she would surprise me at random moments, popping by the mat where Ms. Bomtrauer had left Greta and Emily and Sawyer and me to work on our floor moves to wrap me in a hug or offer a tip or make fun of my less-than-fruitful attempts at grace. At one point, Noe lay on her back and laughed until she cried. I stood over her with my arms folded.

"What?" I demanded. "WHAT?"

"Annabeth," she said. "It's a gym, not a maximum-security prison. You don't have to look so *stern*."

She peeled herself up off the mat and did an impression of me: jaw set, eyebrows knit, planting her hands with a *thwack* and landing with a *clomp*.

"That is *not* how I look," I said.

"Oh, Annabeth," she said. "We'll make a gymnast of you yet."

She straightened my shoulders and turned my hips, showed me how to lift my arms high above my head and rock back slightly before throwing my body forward one limb at a time.

"Noe," a semi-irritable Ms. Bomtrauer called from across the gym. "Your exalted presence is required in Level Nine Land. Annabeth, that's enough cartwheels, I need you to work on your bridge."

"Coming," Noe sang, scampering back to the vault. I

blushed, sheepish at getting in trouble and privately enjoying the shared reprimand.

As the palms of my hands met the coolness of the mat, I thought how lovely it was to feel yourself molded into something better, to feel the motions of your real limbs and muscles inch closer to the perfect version in your imagination. Maybe that was why Noe loved it so much, why she treated the other gymnastics girls like fellow members of a secret society, hugging them and trading obscure lingo in the hall. After practice, I always stayed back with her to stack the heavy mats into a pile and push the equipment to the walls, or we'd go to the Java Bean with Kaylee and Rhiannon and Lindsay, squeezing into a booth by the window and drinking iced cappuccinos until it got dark.

One day at the end of practice, I went to grab Noe's hoodie where she'd forgotten it by the vault and saw a bright red heart sewn inside it, the stitches hidden behind the kangaroo pocket. I stood by the vault with the hoodie in my hands, momentarily stunned. Noe hadn't told me that Steven had sewn a heart into her hoodie, with stitches so tiny and close they looked like a string of kisses.

As I walked across the gym with the hoodie tucked under my arm, my heart thumped in a way I couldn't explain. Somehow, I wished I hadn't seen it. The discovery made me feel strange and guilty, like the time I'd found the antidepressants behind Mom's bathroom mirror. Great love, great pain: both made me uncomfortable, tugging as they did at the corresponding places in myself. I wondered at the startling red of the heart stitched so tightly into the well-worn fabric, at the intimacy and certainty it suggested.

"You forgot this," I said, and tossed it to her.

"Thanks, doll," she said.

15

THE WEEKEND OF THE SENIOR CAMPING trip, we had a gymnastics meet at Gailer College, the sprawling university forty-five minutes from our town. I didn't have a floor routine or bars routine yet, so all I had to do was jump over the vault a couple of times and do a few simple moves on the beam. Noe had forgotten the camera, so we couldn't take pictures like we'd planned. I got restless waiting around the noisy gym for the rest of the day, and tried to go for a walk outside, but the campus was basically a giant parking lot, and when I walked toward a stand of trees I ran into the freeway. I sat on a strip of grass and browsed through the beat-up copy of *How to Survive in the Woods* I always kept in my backpack, until a maintenance person rode up with a weed whacker and the noise forced me back inside.

After the meet, Noe and a bunch of girls from the team wanted to go to the mall to shop for dresses and shoes for the homecoming dance. The mall was right across the freeway from the college, so it wasn't very hard.

"Let's give Annabeth boobs," Noe said, and everyone crowded into Victoria's Secret to hunt for horrifying push-up bras. It was fun to be the center of attention; exhausting, too. When we left the lingerie store, I was drained. As our group drifted to the next shop, I glanced forlornly at the puffy white clouds and sunshine showing through the mall's skylights. It would have been a great day for the forest.

"You look pooped," Mom said when Noe dropped me off at home. "How'd you do?"

"The things I put myself through for Noe," I groaned, and flopped onto the couch.

I meant it to be funny, but Mom didn't laugh.

"She's sure lucky," she said, and waggled my socked foot back and forth before disappearing upstairs.

HOMECOMING WAS A WEEK LATE THIS year, so it landed in early October. Normally, the homecoming dance is in the gym, but one of the Senior Leaders' parents owned a hotel across the parkway from the Botanical Gardens, and they were letting the school have both homecoming and prom in the ballroom for free. It was a good thing, too, because on the day of the dance a pipe burst in the gym ceiling and swamped the floor with an inch of water, and some of the bouncy mats got ruined and the vault was soaked through.

In sophomore year, Noe and I got ready for the dance at my house and took a million silly photos before Mom drove us to the school. We stayed at the dance for only half an hour, then walked to the Jamba Juice in our dresses and high heels, the fall air cool around our bare shoulders. We spent the rest of the evening drinking raspberry smoothies and gossiping about last year's seniors, who were mostly going to Gailer College and mostly drunk out of their minds. That was the night we made our plans for Paris and the dandelion tattoos.

"If I'm still here in three years, crashing my old high school's homecoming dance, please shoot me," Noe had said.

"This time three years from now, we'll have already gone to Paris," I'd answered.

"Do you think you'll still be a virgin?" Noe had said.

"I hope not. What about you?"

"I think so."

"Even after Paris?" I teased.

Noe had nodded. "I want it to be with my forever man."

"I would go for a hot French guy."

"Really?" Noe said.

"The way I imagine it, I'd be sitting on the edge of some beautiful fountain in Paris, and this hot guy would sit next to me, and we'd feel a crackling soul connection, and we'd go drink wine at one of those outdoor cafés and talk for hours, and then we'd kiss in an alley and we'd be so overcome by passion we'd just do it."

"Your dream is to lose your virginity in an alley with a stranger," Noe said.

"It's *romantic*," I'd said, somewhat miffed at Noe's over-looking the crackling soul connection part.

"*I* think you're going to fall madly in love with someone and marry him," Noe said.

I'd rolled my eyes. Noe always wanted me to have the things that made *her* happy; it was annoying sometimes, but mostly it was charming.

"Maybe it's a Freudian thing," Noe said. "You've never met your dad, so you fantasize about a stranger. My parents got married right after high school, so I fantasize about finding my true love."

We'd psychoanalyzed each other all evening, spinning out each other's every feature in the way that only best friends can. When the Jamba Juice closed, we teetered to Noe's house on high heels and fell asleep in front of a movie, both of us bun-dled up on the couch under one blanket.

I wished that this year could be the same, but Noe had ambitions.

"It's our senior year," she said. "We should go all out."

Before the dance, we went to this fancy Italian restaurant in a big group, Noe and Steven and me and some girls from gymnastics. It was frankly kind of exhausting. The restaurant was noisy and crowded, and people kept putting their hands to their ears and saying *"WHAT?"* every time I tried to say some-thing. Steven and I joked around for a while, drawing portraits of people on our napkins, but then Noe noticed what we were doing.

"It's not a Chuck E. Cheese's," she said. "You don't draw on the napkins." She swiped the pen we were sharing and stuck it in her purse. I felt bad for bringing down the tone of her romantic evening, and I could tell Steven did, too. A few minutes later, they got up to make the rounds of other tables. He slipped his arm around her back and didn't even try to tickle her, a boy on conspicuous good behavior.

I got squished in beside Kaylee and Rhiannon, and they kept asking me questions like "Why are you so quiet? Why don't you ever talk?" and "Is it true your mom had you when she was in high school? What happened to your dad?"

I didn't know what to say to them. Even Noe didn't know the whole truth. It all made me so uncomfortable, I couldn't finish my linguine. I pretended to send text messages on my phone until Noe slid onto the leather seat beside me and said, "How are things going at this end of the table? Everyone having fun?"

Things got better at the dance. The ballroom was decorated with streamers and flowers in the E. O. James colors, and the Senior Leaders were handing out Gerbera daisies at the door. Everyone danced in a big group and I didn't have to talk, but in the second hour, they started playing slow songs. Noe and Steven put their arms around each other and got all serious and whispery. It felt weird to lurk around them while they were dancing like that, so I took my purse from the place where I had stashed it and headed outside. I told myself I was going out for fresh air, but the truth was, I was still feeling kind of bad from the restaurant, and I wanted to be alone.

There were too many people going in and out of the big fancy doors at the front of the hotel, laughing and taking photos of themselves next to the potted plants, so I walked around to the parking lot side. I sat on a low concrete stoop next to a buzzing heater vent and took out *How to Survive in the Woods* from my purse.

I'd been sitting there for only a few minutes, feeling the pleasant dampness of the concrete through my dress, when Oliver Mazetti came around the corner, holding a plastic sports bottle in one hand. The back of my neck warmed. Oliver was a senior last year. That summer, he'd worked as a groundskeeper at the Botanical Gardens. We'd said hey a couple of times when I was working at the ice-cream shop, but I hadn't thought about him at all since school started.

"Hey," said Oliver. "Ice-cream girl."

He'd been walking to his car, I guess, but he changed course and walked over to where I was sitting. Oliver didn't even go to E. O. James anymore, but it was kind of a tradition for last year's seniors to crash homecoming. I'd seen a few others inside the dance.

"What are you doing back here?" he said.

"Just taking a break."

Oliver's arms were tanned from working outside all summer, and he had a long, pink scar on the back of one hand from an accident with a pair of hedge clippers. I knew because I'd been working that day and Oliver's manager had come in to borrow our first-aid kit.

Oliver settled himself beside me on the concrete wall. "Whatcha reading?" he said.

I showed him my book.

"You brought a wilderness survival manual to the homecoming dance?" said Oliver.

"Hey, man," I said, "it's a jungle in there."

He laughed, and it felt like the temperature had shot up by a hundred degrees.

"Want some of this?" he said, holding out his sports bottle.

"What is it?"

"Jack Daniel's and Gatorade."

"Classy," I said. "What are you, an alcoholic football coach?"

"You're mean," he said. He bumped my knee with his knee. "I bet you're one of those girls who like the fruity drinks with the little umbrellas."

"Nah," I said. "Hand it over."

My hand was shaking as I took the sports bottle and

squirted the drink into my mouth. What was I doing? Whatever it was, I liked it. Already I could see myself on Noe's bed, telling her everything. *Hey, man, it's a jungle in there.*

"You still working at the Gardens?" I said.

"Three more weeks," said Oliver.

"Then what?"

"Then I'm going to Alaska."

"No shit."

Oliver took a squirt of Gatorade and handed the bottle back to me. "Yeah, a buddy of mine has an uncle up there, he's going to get us on with a crew fishing king crab. Most dangerous job in the world."

"Wow," I said.

"They made this whole TV show about it. Fuckin' sick. It pays like a thousand bucks a week."

"I want to go to Alaska someday."

"That's why you're reading that book, huh. Maybe you can give me some advice. What do I do if a polar bear attacks me?"

"I don't know," I giggled.

"Come on, you're the girl with the book."

"Throw it some king crab."

"I'm not giving my crab to the fucking polar bear, that shit's worth a hundred dollars a pound."

We kept talking like that until the bottle was empty—about Alaska, whose job at the Botanical Gardens sucked worse, impressions of Mr. Beek, the principal, who was the person responsible for getting Oliver expelled last year.

"So are you going back in there or what?" said Oliver.

"I don't know," I said, my cheeks pinkening with the admission that I was open to more exciting possibilities.

"Want to go for a walk?"

"All right."

We slipped off the ledge and started across the grass toward the Gardens. My high-heeled shoes felt tippy and strange on the knobby grass, like walking on the moon.

"Easy there," said Oliver, and slipped an arm around my back.

We crossed the parkway and walked right past the ice-cream shop and into the Gardens. I paused and wrestled my shoes off, clutching Oliver's arm to keep from falling over. I put them on top of a garbage can, which my slightly tipsy brain assured me was a responsible choice of location, where I would be sure not to forget them.

"Want to see something cool?" said Oliver.

I murmured yes. He took my hand and we walked through the damp grass, threading our way between beds of coneflowers and banks of roses. It was strange to think that a month ago, I was here as an employee, sweating in my uniform shirt and scooping cone after cone. So much had already changed since then, and now here I was, on a walk with Oliver, moonlight on my bare arms and neck, having the kind of night you remember forever.

We walked down a path to a backstage part of the garden, with storage sheds and a fleet of golf carts parked under a metal hangar. I'd never been there before, but as a groundskeeper Oliver knew it well.

"It's right over here," Oliver said.

He led me to a small greenhouse, more of a crystalline shed. He opened the door and we stepped inside. It was filled with orchids nodding on wiry green stems. The air was warm and damp and fragrant, like a shower when someone's just turned the water off.

"Pretty cool, right?" said Oliver.

He put his hand on my hip and I made an acquiescing motion. Our mouths met and our tongues began to move against each other like Siamese fighting fish dropped into the same bowl. We did a dreamy stagger from the middle of the orchid house to the wall, and from there a slow collapse to an accommodating stretch of ground.

"Do you want to stop?" Oliver said.

Did I want to stop? No, I wanted to keep going.

"Still okay?" Oliver said. "Still okay?"

"Yes."

Some maneuvering. More maneuvering. An embarrassed mumble from Oliver, an encouraging word from me, and then—

I gasped, and my foot kicked a flowerpot.

"Still okay?"

In response, I kissed him.

The orchids peered down like little faces.

Fallen flowerpots spilled soil on the ground.

Moonlight slanted through a broken section of greenhouse glass.

Oliver tasted just like the waterfall.

17

AT HOME, IN MY BEDROOM, I spun around three times, kissed the orchid I had stolen, and pressed it between the pages of my Spanish-English dictionary.

I lay on my bed and felt the ceiling whirl.

I opened the window and let the night air creep in, let it envelop the older, wiser, worldlier person I had just become.

"SO WHAT'S THE BIG SECRET?" said Noe.

We were sitting on her bed. It was early afternoon, and Noe was still in her pajamas, purple flannel with cows on them. The flowers Steven had given her were on her dresser in a big glass vase. When I looked at them, my whole body fluttered with the memory of orchids. I wasn't used to being the one whose life was more romantic, but last night, for the first time ever, I was pretty sure I had won. I'd been holding on to the news all morning, like a brightly colored button I was smuggling under my tongue. When Noe still wasn't answering texts by one o'clock, I'd called her mom on the landline and she'd gone upstairs to rouse a sleepy Noe out of bed.

"I went to the orchid house with Oliver Mazetti," I blurted.

As soon as I said it, I could feel it all over again—the moonlight, and the dew on my skin, and the low, rumbly, squee-inducing timbre of Oliver's voice when he asked if I was sure I wanted to. My toes curled, and I brought my fists to my mouth and rocked back and forth a little, as if the fact of it was so momentous that to think about it left me physically incapable of staying still.

"Wait, *what*?" said Noe.

"I went outside to cool off, and he walked past the place I was sitting, and we ended up drinking Jack Daniel's and Gatorade and talking *forever*, and then he asked if I wanted to go for a walk, and we snuck into the Botanical Gardens, and he took me to this secret place that only the groundskeepers know about, and we—um . . ." I trailed off, trembling in anticipation of Noe's reaction.

"You made *out* with him?" Noe screeched.

"We did more than that."

It took a second for that to sink in.

"Ohmigod," screamed Noe. "Annabeth, you WHORE!"

She threw a pillow at me. I made a squawk of surprise, and then we both started laughing, a juddering, unstoppable laughter like a machine gone out of control. It filled Noe's bedroom and seemed to rock the entire house. The fact of it was too huge. There was no sensible thing to say.

"I feel like I should ask you questions, but I don't know what to ask," said Noe when she recovered her breath. "Was it thrilling?"

I picked up the pillow she'd thrown at me and hugged it to my chest. "Um. Yes."

"Did he seduce you or did you seduce him?"

"It was a mutual seduction," I said.

We both started cracking up again, the giddiness of the conversation too much for the small bedroom.

"Are you going to see him again?" said Noe. "Or was it, like, a crazy one-night thing?"

The question had been buzzing around in my head all morning. I'd imagined every possible scenario—from never seeing Oliver again and keeping our night at the orchid house as my wildest, most fabulous memory, to starting a whirlwind romance involving three weeks of orchid house escapades before Oliver's tragic departure for Alaska.

"I don't know," I said. "We traded numbers, but it was more of a thanks-for-a-great-night thing than a hey-let's-be-boyfriend-and-girlfriend thing. I don't think we'd have much to talk about."

"Steven and I haven't done *anything*," Noe said. "We tried making out with our shirts off one time, and it was so awkward. We were both like, 'Let's put our shirts back on and play another round of Speed.'"

"What made it awkward?" I said.

"I don't know," said Noe. "Steven's family's really religious, and he was afraid of accidentally doing something wrong or disrespectful. We talked about it for a long time, and he was like, 'I just want to kiss you and bring you lots of flowers and not do things for a long time,' and I was like, 'That's okay with me.'"

I suppressed a smile. Noe had always been skittish about physical stuff, and had kissed her last boyfriend exactly twice. She never seemed to realize that the awkwardness came as much from her as from the boys she dated. It was cute and a little heartbreaking, this inability of Noe's to admit her own apprehension. It made me want to protect her even more.

"Do you feel different?" said Noe.

"Kind of."

"How?"

We lay back on Noe's bed, our bodies blanketed in sunlight.

"It's like . . ." I struggled to find the right metaphor. "When you've spent a lot of time thinking about jumping off a high diving board, and wondering if it will be scary, and if you'll get water up your nose, and then you do it and you're like, 'Okay, I could do that again,' and the next time you see someone do it in a movie you're like, 'I've done that.'"

"I just can't believe it was *last night*. It's so random."

"So perfect," I said.

Outside the window, cicadas were going *chirrrrrr-chirr-chirr-chirr-chirr*. Noe squeezed my hand.

"It feels like everything's *happening*, Bethy. You know what I mean?"

"I know what you mean," I said, and the room seemed to glow and pinken like a flower about to burst into light.

19

"SO, ANNABETH," SAID STEVEN. "WHAT'S this I hear about you sneaking off from the dance?"

We were in the cafeteria, and Noe and I had been telling Steven about our restaurant idea, with the tiny spoons and the order slip where you could specify exactly two and a half ounces of soup so there would never be any waste. Last night, Oliver had texted me when I was still at Noe's house, and we'd pored over the message together—hey—and determined my response, a noncommittal yet encouraging hey ☺. I'd turned off my phone before he could text back, too overwhelmed by the drama of the first exchange to contemplate a second move, or a third.

"Can I tell him?" Noe said to me. "Please?"

"Noe—"

"Annabeth went to the orchid house," she said, waggling her eyebrows on *orchid house* and shimmying her shoulders like a burlesque dancer.

"She got arrested?" said Steven.

"Yes," I said. "Public indecency."

"No," said Noe, "it means she took acid."

"No," I said, "it means I frequented a brothel."

"Actually," Noe said, "Annabeth is a drugged-out criminal prostitute."

"I *knew* it," said Steven, smacking his hand on the table.

I laughed into my milk carton. I had a vision of Noe and me at Northern next year, the cool intellectual table in the cafeteria, trading jokes until they shut down the dinner service and practically had to kick us out. Later, in our dorm room, Noe would chat with Steven on the computer, and I'd stretch out on my bed and recall the details of my latest romantic encounter.

Steven's theater friends came up to our table to talk to him, and soon they'd squeezed onto the benches beside us and were dealing out a card game. Noe hooked her arm through mine.

"Shall we?" she said.

It took me a second to catch her meaning. "Sure," I said.

We got up to make our escape. As we left the crowded cafeteria, Steven's voice wafted after us—"What? What? You guys aren't going to play euchre?"—until we were both doubled over in the laughter of conspirators who can't even remember what the conspiracy is.

* * *

That afternoon after school, I walked to the train tracks. The train tracks are my favorite place in our town. They run along the edge of a psychedelic forest that thrums and buzzes with insect song until you are sure you have crossed into another world. This forest is filled with bee balm and goldenrod and dusty stands of sumac. You can break off a furry red horn and suck the berries for their fuzzy, sour juices and in this manner avoid getting scurvy.

When I got there, the last of the fireflies were bobbing and flashing in tunnels of leaves. I sat against the abandoned car that has been rusting there since Mom was a kid and listened to the freight trains shudder and moan.

I built a little pile of leaves and sticks and gravel, like a shrine to something, I don't know what. All I knew was I felt happy and loved, a trembling leaf on the great big tree of the world. The cicadas mounted their deafening drone around me and I stood up and danced, a private madness overcoming me, the madness of being seventeen and no longer a virgin on the last warm night of fall.

Thank you, I whispered to no one in particular. *Thank you, thank you, thank you.*

A train whistle blew. I bowed and touched the ground, aware of how crazy I must look, and how little, in that moment, I cared.

81

OLIVER STARTED CHATTING ME EVERY night after
school, but we didn't have much to say, and after making vague
plans to get together again before he left for Alaska, the chats
tapered off and then stopped. I was relieved. The truth was,
Oliver himself was almost peripheral to the whole experience.
More intoxicating was the romance of it, the movie-script per-
fection of the evening we'd shared. All week at school, I'd been
buzzing, trying to keep the tremulous brightness of it inside
myself. Now and then, Noe and I would exchange a glance, or
we'd walk home after gymnastics with our arms around each
other's shoulders, feeling the hugeness of things.

When we get our tattoos, we kept saying.

When we have our dorm room.

When we open our restaurant.

I thought of the birdcalls in Mom's book. The birdcall for Noe and Annabeth: *When-we, when-we, when-we.*

21

OCTOBER TURNED COLD THE WEEK before Halloween, just gave up its hold on the summer like a doomed mountain climber letting go of the edge of a cliff. The leaves dropped off the trees and Mom brought our winter box up from the basement, the one with all the hats and scarves and mismatched mittens. Slowly, slowly, the thrill of the orchid house gave way to commonplace things.

In English, we discussed the three forms of irony.

In Media Studies, we dissected the hidden messages in various advertisements.

In gym practice, Noe regaled me with tales of E. O. James gymnasts past and present. There was Lindsay Harris, whose tampon fell out when she lifted her leg for a split in the middle of her beam routine. There was Mindy Chafik, who got drunk before a gym meet and did a spinning projectile vomit from the top of the bars. There was Cassidy LaClaire, who nobody had realized was a cutter until she appeared on the floor in her leotard, a ladder of scars running down each inner thigh. Noe was an expert on these girls and many others. Noe knew every secret, had the inside scoop on every transgression. I listened with a mixture of horror and awe. There were so many ways for a girl to ruin herself, Noe seemed to imply. How lucky we were to be above all of that.

A few days before Halloween, we had a mini meet at the Catholic high school, St. Barnabas. There weren't too many teams there, and everyone from E. O. James got at least one ribbon. Mostly, we huddled on the bleachers and made fun of the St. Barnabas gymnasts, who were matronly and stout and looked like jiggling sides of ham in their pink and white leotards with the St. Barnabas cross on the butt. I got third place for my bar routine, our whole team erupted in applause, and on the bus ride home all Noe could talk about was how *incredible* I was. "You should have seen yourself, Bethy. I wish you could have seen yourself. You looked like a gymnast!"

In Business Math, we learned about compound and simple interest.

In Drama, we acted out scenes from various Shakespeare plays.

In Art, we had a mini opening during the last ten minutes

of class wherein we got to wander around the room looking at one another's self-portraits and discussing their merits among ourselves, although nobody actually did. The art was pretty bad. Most people had done charcoal drawings of themselves, except for Steven, who had done a photomosaic consisting of a thousand tiny pictures of Noe, and Amy McDougall, who had done a pen-and-ink rendition of herself as an anime character, complete with the mile-high legs and miniskirt. And, of course, my bundle of sticks.

Steven and I trailed around the classroom together, peering at the portraits.

"Is that what I think it is?" said Steven.

I squinted at Amy's drawing, which was tacked to the bulletin board in a sea of charcoal faces.

"Panties," said Steven. "You can see her panties."

"Oh," I said. "Oh, wow."

You could see her panties. You actually could.

At the end of the class, we got to collect our self-portraits along with our grade. I saw Amy check the back of her anime drawing and smile. Steven's *Boy with the Rainbow Heart* had a *P* for Pass. My bundle of sticks had a slip of paper underneath with an *R* for Redo.

"This is an outrage," I said as Steven and I walked out of the room. "How can he fail *RAW MATERIALS* but pass anime-panties McDougall?"

"You have to admit that anime-panties displays a fine mastery of the art of shading," said Steven. "I cannot say the same for *RAW MATERIALS*."

"Anime-panties is the visual equivalent of fan fiction," I said. "*RAW MATERIALS* is a raw and powerful gesture."

"*RAW MATERIALS* is a pile of sticks," said Steven. "Lest we forget."

"How can you say that?" I screeched. "You're the one who told me to hand it in. *Ooh, I'm Steven, I've been getting straight A's in art for years.*"

Steven looked pained. "The hallmark of great artists is being misunderstood. That Redo is just a sign that we're on to some heady shit."

We strolled down the hall and came to the bathrooms. I headed for the girls'. Steven followed me. I paused. "You're coming in? It's the girls' bathroom."

"I have to pee too," said Steven.

"So go in the guys' bathroom."

"But we're having a conversation!"

I hovered by the sinks. "Seriously, go away."

"Oh, please, Annabeth. Like nobody's heard you pee before."

"Steven."

"What? I thought we were friends."

"Just because we're friends doesn't mean we need to be pee sisters," I said.

"Pee sisters! Pee sisters!" Steven sang.

He went into a stall, the door swinging free behind him. A few seconds later, I heard a voluminous splashing.

"Come on, Annabeth. Pee with me."

I opened my mouth to scold him, but instead I shrugged and went into a stall myself. Steven talked the whole time.

"You know that unisex bathrooms are the new thing. In fifty years, our grandchildren are going to think we're so old-fashioned because we grew up with segregated toilets."

I started talking too, mostly to cover up the sound.

"There will be pee riots," I said. "The gender symbols will be ripped from bathroom doors and burned in public squares."

"Exactly!" said Steven.

"Thousands were arrested in the great pee riots of 2024," I said in my best news-announcer voice. "But in the referendums of 2025, bathroom suffrage was achieved at last."

We joined at the sink to wash our hands.

"Pee sisters?" I said as we exited the bathroom.

Steven made a cockeyed salute. "Pee sisters forever," he said.

We came upon Noe a few steps later. She was walking down the hall with Kaylee and Lindsay from the gym team.

"You guys looks awfully pleased with yourselves," she said.

"We're pee sisters," I said.

Kaylee and Lindsay exchanged a look.

"Excuse me?" said Noe.

Steven giggled. "We subverted the dominant paradigm of gender-specific bladder relief."

"We brought an antidisestablishmentarianist perspective to bear on the issue of male/female urination roles," I said.

"O-kay," Noe said. It was strange to see her like this, performing for Kaylee and Lindsay instead of joining in on our fun. It gave me a curious urge to poke her. The other day in gym practice, I'd overheard Noe telling them that she and Steven had come *this close* to doing it the last time she was at his house, which struck me as a pretty big elaboration considering what she had told me. Sometimes I forgot that Noe's self-confidence had limits. When it came to other girls, she could be downright insecure.

"Speaking of gender roles," Noe said to Steven, "you're driving us to the movies at eight o'clock tonight."

He seemed to sober up. "Yes, ma'am," Steven said.

He fell into step beside her, hooking his pinky finger through hers like they always did. I groaned inwardly. Surely, Noe wasn't worrying about what Lindsay and Kaylee thought of Steven. She was *Noe*. Who cared what anyone thought?

"You two are too cute," said Lindsay Harris, she of the fallen-out tampon.

It was jarring to hear Lindsay Harris commenting on Noe and Steven in a familiar way, as if they belonged to her. *What are you doing?* I almost said. *That's mine.*

As we walked down the hall, I found myself at the back of the group, and wondered how that had happened.

"Does anyone know what lunch is?" said Noe.

I tried to tell her it was spaghetti and slaughter balls, but everyone was talking so loudly I don't think she heard.

22

BOB WAS LISTENING TO HIS audiobook again when I went in for my second appointment. He was doing something on the computer and didn't notice me slip into the room until I'd been sitting in the Sorting Chair for almost five minutes. I didn't try to catch his attention. I rested my head on my chin and listened to the story. It was pretty dumb—something about fairies and swords and people trapped in ice—but I found myself getting sucked in anyway. Bob realized I was there when we both laughed out loud at something the Jocular Wizard said.

"Annabeth!" said Bob. "When did you come in?"

"What book is that?" I said.

He blushed and rummaged in his desk for the CD case. He passed it to me. *Kingdom of Stones*. It had an unfortunate rendering of a bawdy wench on the front, with a landscape of cairns and crags behind her.

"Cool," I said.

He reached for the CD player and clicked it off.

"Do you want to see my food journal?" I said.

Bob flipped through the lined pages and added a few things up on a chunky calculator that looked like it had been rescued from the 1980s.

"Wow," he said. "Very thorough."

I smiled, but I felt guilty. The truth is, I hadn't really been keeping track of my food. It was too much trouble. Instead, Noe had helped me fill in the past month's worth of columns yesterday afternoon in English.

"How about an omelet for Monday?" she'd said. "That's protein-y."

"Can I have hash browns too?"

Hash browns, Noe noted on the page.

"How about some toast?"

Toast, 2 pcs, Noe wrote.

"Oh, and green beans."

"For breakfast?"

"I should have a vegetable, shouldn't I?"

Noe shook her head. "He'll smell a rat."

"Are we almost finished?"

"Yup. Just need Tuesday lunch. I'm thinking a burrito, a salad, and a glass of milk."

"You're too good at this," I'd said.

Noe cackled, and wrote down *Rice Krispie square* for good measure.

"The numbers look fine," said the nutritionist. "I guess I can't make you keep coming. But if there is ever something you feel like talking about, you're welcome anytime."

He smiled one of his sad smiles and gave me a pizza coupon.

I held it in my fingers, feeling like there was something I was supposed to say. There wasn't, so I stuffed it into my pocket and left.

AT LUNCH, I WAVED THE PIZZA coupon at Noe and Steven.

"I'm off the hook with Señor Bob," I said.

"That's no fun," said Steven. "You didn't even get to show him your self-portrait."

"He loved the journal," I said to Noe. "The Rice Krispie square was a masterstroke."

She put her arm around my shoulder. "Anytime, doll. Anytime."

That afternoon, I went to the Java Bean with Noe and Steven, and Oliver walked in. I had to go hide in the bathroom while Noe ordered a coffee for me.

"Was that your orchid house lover?" said Steven when I came back. "He ordered a very large cruller."

I groaned and sank down in our booth until I was practically under the table, and Noe had to drag me back up. "Leave her alone, Steven."

"What? What? He's a big guy. Big guys eat big donuts. Did I say something weird?"

Noe put her hand over his mouth to shut him up before I died of mortification. "Just. Stop. Talking," she said.

I guess the movies had gone okay. Noe and Steven seemed better than ever. I snuck a glance at them across the table, quietly pleased with the way they snuggled together, matching hearts drawn on both their hands in red ink. It was good to see two people I liked loving each other. It filled me with vicarious warmth.

I picked up a wooden stir stick and waved it in the air above their heads.

"What are you doing?" Noe said.

"Anointing your union."

They giggled and bowed their heads, giddy smiles creasing their faces while I dipped the stick in coffee and shook it over them again and again.

It felt like Oliver should have been in Alaska already, but I saw him again at the Walmart, and again from the car window, walking down the street with a Super Gulp from the 7-Eleven, while Mom and I were driving to Nan's house for dinner.

Finally, I saw online that he had left for Alaska, so I didn't have to worry about him anymore. On Halloween, Noe, Steven, and I dressed up like pirates and hung out at Noe's house handing out candy. Afterward, we went on a long, rambling walk around the neighborhood, through the graveyard, and past the big construction site on the edge of Lorian Woods and back through the park where the ground was wet and squishy and the chestnut tree had lost its leaves.

When we got back to Noe's house I waited, gazing at my shoes, while Noe pressed Steven up against his car and they kissed for what felt like forever. After a while, I glanced up. I could see the top of Steven's head poking up above Noe's swirls of hair. They didn't seem to be kissing anymore, but their foreheads were pressed together. Noe said something and I heard Steven laugh. It was just a scrap of laughter, but it stood out like a spray of pink flowers on the side of a muddy road. It had a note of delighted wonder, of celebration at one's own dumb luck.

Noe came speed-walking up the driveway as he drove away, her cheeks flushed.

"He said it," she blurted.

I hooked my arm through hers and hurried into the house with her.

"Noe," I exclaimed. "Noe!"

Steven had said *I love you*. And Noe had said it back. In her room, we danced around in our pirate costumes.

"Everything's happening," we said over and over, until it turned into a magic spell, an incantation, sweeping us out of Noe's bedroom and into the great rushing hugeness of the rest of our lives.

24

THE SECOND WEEKEND OF NOVEMBER was Gym Expo Northeast. It wasn't a meet, exactly, but a big gathering where you could take workshops, watch demonstrations by university gymnastics, cheerleading, and dance teams, shop for fancy leotards, and collect free samples of energy bars. Noe and the other advanced girls had raised money to go last year. I'd helped out at the car wash, standing on the corner waving a cardboard sign. In practice on Thursday, it was all anyone could talk about. They were going to leave on Friday after class, and stay in a hotel for two nights, and eat in restaurants, and on the way home they were going to stop at the giant mall in Baxterville and go shopping.

I spent the weekend raking leaves with Mom, first at our house and then at Nan's. As we raked, we talked about all things Northern.

"It's so silly they schedule campus visits for December," she said. "You should see it right now. The forest is a blaze of endless color, and the air smells like . . ." She trailed off. "I wish I could get the time off so we could go up together."

She told me all about the dormitory where she and Pauline had lived in their freshman year, and the Ecosystems class where the professor, Dr. Clarke, assigned them to spend all day in a tree, observing the weather and wildlife.

"You're going to love it, Annabean. It's a small school. You get to know all the professors. I'll never forget Dr. Clarke's class. She was such a genius, so inspiring. I wanted to be just like her."

I felt a twinge when Mom said that, like the monster had plucked a string inside me, just to remind me it was there.

"I think Noe and I are going to go on exchange to Paris in our second year," I said to cover my anxiety. "Either that or move off campus. Max said we could have his trampoline."

"Oh, lordy," said Mom. "Now there's a crucial piece of furniture."

Later, Mom stopped by my room to ask if I wanted to go to a movie. "What happened to your homecoming dress?" she said, stepping inside to finger the dirt-stained satin. I'd taken it out of my closet along with a few others to try on, like I sometimes did when I was feeling bored. My heart began to hammer.

"Two words," I said. "Noe. Somersaults."

Mom let out an amused snort. "What would homecoming be without somersaults? Too bad about the dress, though. It was a nice one."

After she wandered out again, I folded the dress into a ball and hid it in my bottom drawer. It had other stains she hadn't noticed—that I noticed myself only after she left the room. I couldn't wait until Noe came back so I could tell her a funny story about the whole almost-disaster. *It was the somersaults, Mom, I swear!*

I sat on my bed and smiled to myself, remembering, until Mom called that it was time to leave for the theater.

25

ON MONDAY, NOE AND KAYLEE AND Lauren and Rhiannon came to school with matching water bottles with GYM EXPO NORTHEAST on the side, and matching bracelets from the big mall they had stopped at on the way home. Apparently, they'd had a crazy time at the hotel. They snuck into the pool after hours and got caught by the cute night manager, and Kaylee said, "Sorry, sir, we were just so hot and bothered." At our lunch table, they kept laughing about it and doing impressions while Kaylee pretended to be embarrassed. "I meant to say we were hot and *bored*! I can't help what comes out of my mouth late at night, guys, you know I'm a spazz."

Noe had taken an advanced beam workshop with a former

Olympic gymnast, Sphinx Lacoeur. Afterward, he had led her aside and asked about her plans for college. She reported the conversation breathlessly.

"I was like, 'No plans!' and he said, 'You're from E. O. James, right?' and I said, 'Um, yes,' and he said, 'Have you heard that Gailer College is getting a gymnastics team next year?' and I said, 'No,' and he said, 'I'm coaching, and I intend to take the team to nationals,' and then he looked into my eyes and said, 'Noe, what can I do to convince you to be a River Rat?'"

Noe looked so happy: blushing and breathless, like a bride, or a princess. I shot her a questioning look.

"Campus visits are going to be so fun," said Kaylee. "My brother promised he'd get us into the Alpha Delta Phi tiki party, but we need to get orange bikinis."

They all squeezed each other's hands in the middle of the table.

"I can't wait," said Noe. "Three weeks!"

Joyous squealing. The plan had clearly been brewing since at least Sunday.

I could imagine them talking about it on the drive home from the Gym Expo, everyone crammed into the car with all their new loot.

Don't panic, I thought to myself. *Don't panic.*

I started to wrap my sandwich in a napkin.

"What's Annabeth doing?" Kaylee said.

The gym girls had long since given up on trying to get me to talk and taken to asking Noe instead. The truth is, I preferred this arrangement. Noe was so much better at explaining me than I was.

"Annabeth's spirit animal is a squirrel," Noe said. "She hates throwing things out."

"I'm saving it for later," I protested, folding the napkins around the remains of my food so that it formed a tidy white package. I tucked the packet into my backpack and zipped it up, blushing slightly under Kaylee's gaze. I didn't like to have my rituals watched. Noe was used to them, others not so much. For this reason, I avoided eating lunch with new people.

"She's so cute," Kaylee said, and everyone laughed.

I tried to catch Noe's eye again—*You're just having fun with the Sphinx Lacoeur thing, right?*—but a couple of freshmen from the choir came up to ask her a question, and then the bell rang for our next class.

26

I SPENT MY NEXT TWO CLASSES trying not to fall apart.

Outside the window, the first flurries of winter were falling. I watched the flakes dust the soccer field, a thin, fuzzy layer of white like a consolation prize for actual snow.

"Ms. Schultz," roared Mr. Genanotron. "Will you please read the next paragraph out loud?"

Suddenly, I was in ninth grade again, too small and too quiet and afraid of everything, my heart beating like a rabbit's every time anyone looked at me, certain that everyone could tell; that they could look at me and see all the slimy things crawling around in there like worms inside a compost bin.

Dead inside and coming to life only in the moments that Noe alighted beside me, like a bike light that lights up and flashes only when someone is turning the pedals, like a radio that fritzes and statics unless calmed by the right hand.

Mr. Genanotron was staring at me, and people were starting to snicker.

Oh, to be a snowflake, a blade of grass, a bird, a chunk of concrete. Anything but what I was: half human, half disease. Half things that yearned to grow and live, half thing that craved to die.

Gailer College wouldn't be so bad, I thought to myself. *It wouldn't be so bad.*

"I don't know where we are," I said.

"Speak up," Mr. Genanotron barked.

"I don't know where we are."

21

"ARE YOU COMING TO GAILER FOR campus visits?" said Noe. "Kaylee needs to let her brother know how many tickets to get for the tiki party."

She was in full Noe planning mode, making lists in her notebook, sorting out carpools and other logistics. Her day planner was splayed open on the table. On the days in which I'd mentally inserted our road trip to Northern University, she'd penned in a meeting with Sphinx Lacoeur, a Gailer College River Rats hockey game, and an orange bikini–shopping expedition at the mall.

I had been planning this whole confrontation—*What about Northern? What about our dorm room? What about Paris?*—but as I watched her scribble another item onto her agenda, the indignation drained out of me. It was dangerous to accuse Noe of anything. *What do you mean?* she would say, her voice sharpening. *I never agreed to anything.* Even worse was the creeping suspicion I had that she'd be right. I'd extrapolated a few fun conversations into a full-blown plan. It was wishful thinking, and sort of pathetic. Still, it hurt that she wouldn't even acknowledge my disappointment.

"Probably," I said. "I'm probably coming."

"Good girl," said Noe, and wrote my name down on her list.

I hesitated. "What are you doing after this? Want to come over?"

"I can't," Noe said. "I'm having coffee with Darla."

"Who's Darla?"

"Steven's mom."

She said it as if I ought to know, like I would naturally keep track of the names of her boyfriends' parents.

"Why are you having coffee with Steven's mom?" I said.

"We hang out sometimes," said Noe. "She's really sweet. She wants me to sing in her choir."

Noe had crazy notions about things. Sometimes I forgot how different we were. Then she would paint her fingernails pink and announce she was *having coffee with Darla*, and it would hit me all over again.

The Venn diagram was a startling place, if you ventured out of that place in the middle and into the nonoverlapping zones.

THE NEXT MORNING, THERE WAS A meeting in the cafeteria for all the seniors. The guidance counselor, Ms. Hack, gave a little speech and passed around forms we had to fill out saying which school we were going to visit during our days off, and then there was a presentation by some people from Gailer College. They handed out free candy bars and showed a Power-Point of the new athletic facilities and talked about all the exciting activities they had planned for campus visit week, and Noe and all the others who were planning to go there cheered and clapped.

In Art, Steven poked me. "Are you okay?" he said.

"Why?"

"You look . . . blank. When I look like that, Ricardo says I am presenting a negative affect."

"You *never* seem negative. I don't even know why they think you're depressed."

"That's because I have Noe now. I really think she cured me. My mood journal has been all tens since June seventeenth."

I sighed. In my head, I was saying good-bye to the Campus Outdoors Club, and the national park, and the long drive with the pit stop at Smoothie Town, and the dorm room with the Gulört rug and the goldfish bowl. The form was in my backpack, with *Gailer College* penciled into the appropriate field.

"Are you sure you're not anemic?" said Steven. "I think Noe's anemic. What if you guys ate grain-fed beef? It's *almost* the same as grain."

I wondered if Steven knew about Noe's emergency-puking thing. The other day, she'd done it for the first time in a long while. The first time that I knew of, anyway. "Did you eat that soup?" she'd said. "Did you know it had chicken broth? Why do they call it Potato Vegetable if what they really mean is Potatoes in Torture Juice?"

"Where are you going for campus visits?" I asked Steven to change the subject.

"NYU," he said.

"Aren't you going to miss Noe?"

"Oh, terribly. It's going to be great. We'll pine for each other all week, and have dazzling weekends of ecstatic reunion. I'm going to get us a family membership to the Museum of Modern Art."

I put my head on the desk and tried not to wail.

At lunch, the tables were littered with plastic orange bracelets that the Gailer College people had left behind, and coupons for free admission to the River Rats game. Whoever had printed them had done the punctuation wrong: RIVER RAT'S. I stuffed a coupon into the bottom of my backpack.

I probably wouldn't have joined the Campus Outdoor Club anyway.

After all, Noe hated camping.

29

AT HOME, MOM FROWNED AT THE form she had to sign but said nothing. We went to Nan's house for dinner, watched a *Masterpiece* show, and played a few rounds of Scrabble. I thought I was off the hook, but on the drive home the words Mom had been suppressing since the afternoon bubbled out of her.

"Are you sure, Annabeth? You should visit Northern. You can stay in Ava's dorm."

"What's wrong with Gailer College?" I said.

Outside the car window, glowy lights of strip malls. We drove past the fortune-teller and the factory outlet mall and the Flying Saucer restaurant where you can get eggs and toast for $2.99. Mom turned the radio down.

"This doesn't have anything to do with Noe, does it?" Mom said.

The Flying Saucer restaurant was a tinny movie prop in the rearview mirror. It really is shaped like a flying saucer; you can pretend to be an alien looking out at the town while you are eating your breakfast.

"No," I said. "Noe has nothing to do with it. I don't get what's wrong with Gailer College."

"There's nothing wrong with Gailer," said Mom. My cousin Max was going there, so she had to be a little careful with what she said. "I just want to make sure you're not passing up Northern because of Noe."

"It's a good school," I said stoutly. "I'll save so much money living at home."

"You know Nan's offered to pay for housing."

"Well, this way she won't have to."

We drove in silence for a moment or two.

"I thought Noe was going to apply to Northern," Mom said for the second time since we'd gotten in the car.

"I already told you. The gym coach pretty much begged her to go to Gailer. He's going to get her a scholarship and everything."

"That's great for her, but what about you?"

I made an irritated sound, like *What are you even* talking *about?*

"You let Noe lead the way in so many areas. I *see* you doing it. And I see you retreating from things you love because she's not interested in them."

My head was starting to ache. "I don't retreat from things," I said.

"You used to be my happy nature girl, and now you're talking about going to school in a shopping mall. Frankly, I think you'd hate Gailer College, and I think you *know* you'd hate it, but you're too—*stuck*—on Noe to do what you really want."

"I'm not *stuck*," I said. My voice was getting shrill.

"You don't seem to have any other friends, you haven't been out with any boys since Jonathan Wellsey in ninth grade, and—"

"What do you know?" I screeched. "What do you even *know*?"

That got her attention. "You *are* seeing a boy?"

"No," I said, but it was too late. She'd detected something in my tone.

"Annabeth, is there something you're not telling me? If there is a boy, I want to meet him."

I stiffened my face. "There isn't a boy."

That only made it worse. I could see her mentally working through the possibilities. *She says there's no boyfriend, and yet—*

Mom swung her eyes off the road to look at me. "Are you having *sex*?" she squawked.

"None of your business," I said, but there was no way to stop the blush that leaped to my cheeks.

"If you are, I want to know."

"I said, *none of your business.*"

That last statement, I shouted. She glanced at me a second time before glaring back at the road.

"Something's really going on with you, isn't it, Annabeth," she muttered.

"I didn't ask you to have me," I said.

30

IN THE HOUSE, MOM SLAMMED AROUND the kitchen making herself a plate of food, which she carried upstairs to her room. I shook some cereal into a bowl, but when I went to get the milk I realized we were out. I grabbed my wallet.

"I'm going to the corner store," I shouted up the stairs. "We're out of milk."

The latter sentence came out bursting with accusation, as if all that was wrong in my life came down to her failure to feed me. I made sure to slam the door on my way out of the house.

When I left the convenience store with the milk jug under my arm, the blue of twilight had deepened into ink. The street was quiet. The porch lights were on and I could see TVs through the curtains of houses.

I walked past the liquor store and past the big drugstore where a weary attendant in a rust-colored apron was slamming the shopping carts into one another and shoving them into their metal corrals for the night.

I thought of Noe and Steven with hearts sewn into their clothes, and brought my wrist to my mouth and bit it.

I thought of the photograph of my mother holding me up while I leaned over the railing to reach for the mist that rose from the waterfall, anchoring herself to the concrete while I strained toward the rushing water.

A breeze fluttered up my shirt. My feet were sore and sweaty inside my running shoes.

Stop looking at me like that, I said inside my head, although I couldn't say exactly who I was saying it to.

THAT NIGHT I COULDN'T FALL ASLEEP. I kept stewing and stewing, carrying on the argument with Mom inside my head. It wasn't fair, that happy-nature-girl comment.

All I could think about was the time I was thirteen. I had just discovered the box full of Mom's old wilderness books in our basement and read *How to Survive in the Woods* cover to cover, and now I was ready for adventure. I imagined myself tromping through the forest, victorious, stoic, hardy, capable. I imagined myself walking from my back door all the way to the North Pole.

It was a day or two after eighth-grade graduation, and the summer hadn't yet turned bad. I'd dragged Mom's old tent out of the basement, and the curious, musty sleeping bag and camping mat. In my room, I packed a sweater, a hat, extra socks, and the rechargeable flashlight Mom made me keep plugged into the wall in case of a power outage.

"Hey, Mom?" I'd said when my pack was ready. "I'm going camping. I'll be back on Sunday."

Camping. I might as well have said I was going to go pick up strange men outside the Thunderbird Casino. The flurry that word caused!

My backpack: unzipped and picked apart, my perfectly adequate supplies declared to be insufficient.

My ability to survive in the woods for two nights questioned, unknown dangers emphasized.

Nan was over, using our computer to look up cake recipes for my cousin Ava's birthday. She'd come upstairs to see what the fuss was about.

"What's all this?"

"I'm going camping."

"Are you going to let her go with only *crackers*, Leslie?" That's Nan, holding up a box of Wheat Thins.

"You're leaving out the rest of the food," I'd protested, motioning at the hard-boiled eggs I'd bundled up in paper towels.

"Annabeth," said Mom. "You know that's not enough for two days."

I waved the plant ID book at her. "The whole point is to supplement with wild things. Milkweed. Sumac. Raspberries."

"Raspberries!" said Nan. "Leslie, she can't go a whole weekend on raspberries."

I should have left a note. Forty-five minutes of bitter negotiation later, they'd driven me to the regional park, where there are official campsites, and a ranger who checks to make sure that you paid, and all sorts of old people sitting outside their trailers on folding chairs drinking cans of off-brand soda. They made me bring an emergency whistle, and a cooler full of sandwiches and fruit and little foil-wrapped packages of Nan's cabbage rolls. My two nights in the forest were reduced to one. One night at the regional park, in the hot dog–smelling air.

If Nan hadn't been there, I would have said a whole lot more to Mom than I did.

Like *How can you do this to me?*

And *If I was a boy you'd let me.*

And *You of all people should understand.*

The things I couldn't say out loud with Nan in the car, I said with my eyes instead. I knew that Mom caught every one by the way she looked back at me in the rearview mirror.

"Annabeth," she said, and I shook my head.

I felt like I was swimming through a school of jellyfish: my whole body prickled and burned. We crept along the asphalt ring road, past the enormous Coleman tents with people barbecuing, until we came to the campsite the ranger had assigned me, number fourteen. It was under some scrubby maple trees. There was a fire ring with a dirty grate propped up over it, and the half-burned remains of someone's cardboard beer box underneath. Mom and I barely spoke as we set up the tent. Someone in a nearby campsite had a radio playing top-forty hits. Another radio was broadcasting the baseball game. As we drove the tent stakes into the ground, an unspoken *I hate you* sizzled between us like a coal.

"Well, I think Annabeth's very adventurous," Nan kept saying. "How many thirteen-year-old girls go on camping trips alone?"

"It's not really camping," I'd grumbled.

"And you have your own little water spout. Look at that."

As we unrolled the camping mat and sleeping bag, Nan wandered off to meet the people in the neighboring campsite.

"Will you keep an eye on my granddaughter?" I heard her saying. "She's camping out all by herself."

Mom and I stood across from one another in front of the car, enveloped in bitter silence. I wouldn't meet her eyes.

"Great campsite," I said. "Think I'll see any stars with all those streetlights?"

"Someday we'll go on a real camping trip."

"I was going to go on a real camping trip this weekend."

We didn't say another word. We only stood there, on the

packed dirt where nothing grew, while the baseball announcer's voice clamored through the thin scrim of trees.

"Annabeth," called Nan. "Come here and meet your neighbors. They've invited you over for supper, isn't that nice?"

I shot Mom a look and started dismantling the tent.

"Take me home," I growled.

I could see on Mom's face that there was something terrible going on inside her, but in my anger it never occurred to me that she was being anything other than selfish and unreasonable.

On the car ride home, Nan had kept patting her hand.

I didn't know then.

I didn't know, and now she wanted to call me her happy nature girl, and tell me to go three hundred miles away on my own, to the very place where the whole ugly mess of my life had started, without even Noe to make it okay.

IT FELT LIKE THE HOUSE WAS filled with paint fumes: instant migraine when you walked in the door. Mom and I avoided each other's eyes and timed our comings and goings to avoid intersection in the kitchen or hall. My head swarmed with equal parts guilt and indignation. Guilt for shutting her out. Indignation at the suggestion that Noe was anything less than my dearest friend in the world.

One day I came home to find a box of condoms on my bed, and a pamphlet titled *What Is Consent?*

As I skimmed it, my cheeks burned with something I tried to convince myself was mortification, but knew to be heartbreak instead.

Mom worried about boys. The first time it emerged that I had kissed one, she made me practice shouting *No!* and kneeing her in the groin until we both started crying.

Personally, I have never required the knee, although God help the poor fool who incites me to deploy it.

Oliver had been a sweet and respectful person in that department, and as I sat on my bed, I wished I could break ranks for long enough to tell Mom that one thing, just that.

The worst part of fighting is the moment you realize the other person is really hurting. It's pretty impossible to keep going after that.

33

I APOLOGIZED TO MOM.

I really cannot stand to see her hurting because of something I said or did.

We spent her birthday going for a hike in the forest, like we used to do all the time when I was younger. It had rained the night before, and the woods smelled fresh and wet and cold.

Later, Uncle Dylan and Aunt Monique and Nan came over and we sat in the kitchen eating a strawberry angel food cake Nan had made. "Leslie says you're thinking about visiting Ava at Northern," Uncle Dylan said. "She'd love to see you."

My uncle Dylan has a ginger mustache and grayish-blue eyes. He used to play on the E. O. James hockey team, and now he has a construction business. My aunt Monique grew up in Chippewa, and now she is a kindergarten teacher. When I was little, I spent a lot of time at their house, playing with my cousins Ava and Max and watching movies on their big TV. I had my own bed there, and the same number of presents at Christmas. Uncle Dylan came to my soccer games and school recitals with Mom so I wouldn't have a smaller audience representation than the other kids.

I love Uncle Dylan. In some ways, it was harder to let him down than Mom.

"I'll pay for the bus ticket," Uncle Dylan said. "How about that?"

I nod-shrugged. My cousin Max had sold me his old Honda last summer, but it was unreliable at the best of times and even I wasn't stubborn enough to insist on driving it all the way to Northern alone.

Uncle Dylan ruffled my hair. "Thattagirl."

I was on the couch after dinner, watching TV with a cup of tea, when I overheard Mom and Nan whispering in the kitchen.

"Leslie, she's too skinny."

"She's tall, Ma."

"You weren't skinny like that when you were seventeen."

"Scott was."

A horrible silence. Evil spirits invoked. Moments later,

the industrious clanging of pots and pans, as if to drive them away. Nan came out to the living room to say good-bye, and we talked for a few minutes, stupid stuff about school and gymnastics and the TV show I was watching. Mom stayed in the kitchen, putting away the rest of the cake.

Upstairs, later, I stepped onto the old pink scale in the bathroom. I was light as a feather but heavier, heavier, heavier than the sea.

I WOKE UP IN THE HOLE.

This happened sometimes.

The trapdoor swung open and there was nothing I could do.

Someone had sprayed fake snow on the windows at the Burger King. The funeral parlor had a wreath of bloodred holly on its door. The cafeteria at school was still hung with fake cobwebs. Due to budget cuts it was doubling as snow.

In Business Math I was a zombie.

In Art I stared at Steven's pencil as it wound its way around the page.

In gymnastics I couldn't stand the harsh fluorescent lights or the chirping voices of the girls who gossiped as they did their stretches and ran through their moves on the beam. Ms. Bomtrauer was on my case about my floor routine. I found myself clamping my teeth in irritation at every reminder to point my toes or lift my chin up when I finished a round-off.

"What are you doing?" Noe said, surprising me by the bench where our backpacks were piled.

"I'm taking a break," I said.

"Bullshit," said Noe. "Back to the mat."

Her "team captain" mode was not without irony, but the briskness still grated. I wasn't used to Noe treating me like another distractable girl who needed managing, instead of the best friend that I was. I followed her across the gym. On the floor, I went through my moves halfheartedly. Since overhearing Mom and Nan in the kitchen, I'd felt haunted and shaken. That morning at breakfast, Mom had pushed a bottle of vitamin pills at me.

"Nan wants you to take these," she'd said.

The vitamin pill had stuck in my throat. It took three glasses of water to push it all the way down. All morning it seemed to dig inside me like a seed, thrusting little roots all through my stomach, sucking up my energy. By lunchtime, it felt like a vine had grown inside me, and an enormous black fruit, cold and bulbous, feeding off me to make itself grow.

As I planted my hands and thrust my legs into the air, I felt a spot of pain where the vitamin pill was still digging. Noe watched me, hands on perfectly rounded hips.

"Shoulders back," Noe said. "Put some effort into it. And take that sweater off."

"I'm cold."

Did I look like him? The thought appalled me. A sweater wasn't enough to hide under. A cave would be the best.

"You're not going to be able to wear a sweater at our gym meets," said Noe, "so you'd better get used to it."

"They should insulate these things," I grumbled.

After practice, I helped Noe push the beam and vault against the back wall and pile the mats into a neat stack. She chattered the whole time, analyzing this girl's beam routine and that girl's troubles with handstands.

"Alicia Morrow was driving me crazy. The girl couldn't be any clumsier on vault if she was a pack mule."

I half listened, making appropriate noises of shock, disapproval, and sympathy.

"Are you okay?" Noe said. "You're so spacey today."

"I'm just tired," I said.

I wondered what it would be like to be a person who felt strong and even every day, who didn't fall into these craters where everything was too bright.

Noe lifted the last mat onto the pile with a grunt. "You need to get that round-off nailed in time for the meet," she said.

As we walked out of the gym, Noe continued her gym babble. Ms. Bomtrauer had ordered a new vault to replace the one that got damaged in the flood. Kaylee Ito couldn't tell the difference between a split leap and a stag, despite constant coaching. Suddenly, everything about Noe seemed irritating to me. The way she cut her food into tiny pieces that were never allowed to touch. The way she bought new binders every year instead of reusing the old ones. The way she sucked up to teachers and coaches and choir directors, fawning over them and insisting that everyone around her do the same. The way she clucked over the gymnastics girls like a mother hen, braiding hair and correcting posture and secretly criticizing everyone behind their backs. The way she waited for Steven after class, claiming him like a child she was picking up from nursery school. The way she showered you with attention when it was convenient for her, only to withdraw it when you needed it the most.

Part of being in the hole was that things I normally didn't mind became unbearable to me.

"Can we not talk about gymnastics?" I burst out.

"If you didn't want to work, you shouldn't have joined the team," clucked Noe. "It's not a social club."

She was so serious since the Gym Expo, all *discipline* and *commitment* and *sports nutrition* and *electrolytes*. She'd started carrying around this textbook called *The Science of Gymnastics* that Sphinx had apparently recommended, and talking about majoring in kinesiology.

"It's not that," I said. "It's not about that."

"Then what is it about?"

I had promised myself I would not bring it up, but the angst that was swarming inside me needed an outlet.

"I thought we were going to Northern together," I exploded. "I thought we were going to be roommates."

It was humiliating to say it out loud, like admitting to having some creepy disease. I could see my utter dependence on her showing through like a badly concealed case of acne. For the second time within the hour, I wished I could do the world a favor and crawl into a cave. That way everyone would be rid of me—Noe, my mom, maybe even myself.

"Tell me more," said Noe in a reasonable voice.

I recognized this tactic from the last time I'd aired this kind of grievance. Noe's strategy when it came to arguments was to let you rant and babble until you felt so shrill and hysterical you willingly retracted whatever charges you had brought against her. Still, I fell for it every time.

"We've been planning it forever. We even named our freaking goldfish. And then you come back from the gym thing and announce you're going to Gailer, and you don't even ask how I *feel*."

We came to the bench in front of the flagpole but didn't

sit down. The wretchedness of last night was surging through me. Industrious clanging of pots and pans. I opened my mouth again. "I know you're going to say that plans change and you never promised anything, but it's more than that. Sometimes I feel like our friendship is this leaky boat, but nobody's allowed to admit the boat is leaking. We just sit there with our feet getting wet, but I can't say, *Hey, my feet are wet*, because you'll throw me overboard."

"Nobody's throwing you overboard," said Noe calmly. "You're having a bad day."

"I thought we were going to be roommates," I said, my voice taking on a panicked edge as it hit me that I was going to have to room with a total stranger.

Noe put her hands on my shoulders. "Plans change, my dear. I didn't know what I wanted back then."

"You can do gymnastics at Northern, too," I said.

"It's not just gymnastics. I don't *want* to go to a tiny school in the middle of nowhere. I don't care about the hiking trails and the canoe club, or whatever. I want to be somewhere with shoe stores. We're not married, Annabeth. You're being insane." Steven appeared fresh from the theater. "Ladies," he said.

"Steveous!" Noe exclaimed and ran to embrace him, her laughter a pointed cue that the conversation was over.

I waited by the flagpole while they went through their several-times-daily ritual of kisses and whispers, a process that had grown considerably more elaborate since their declarations on Halloween night. Angry thoughts were still running through my head. I wondered what Steven would think if he knew what Noe had said about his best friend, Dominic, after they'd run into him at the Pita Pit: "Oh my God, Annabeth, it was horrible. He was, like, this creepy little mole person. He came and stood right by our table and said, 'So, Noe, what are your intentions with Steven?' in this annoying theater voice, and then Steven got all mad when I didn't make room for him to sit with us."

I'd had a class with Dominic last year. He was probably the shyest person I'd ever met. It was cruel of Noe to call him a creepy little mole, just plain cruel.

The skinny tree the school planted on Earth Day last year was shivering in the wind, its leaves dried up into tiny yellow curls like fingernails.

"Annabeth," Steven called. "You look like you're going to cry."

"She's having a bad day," Noe said, throwing a consoling arm around my shoulder.

"Really?" said Steven. "What happened?"

"Gymnastics problems," I said. "Ms. Bomtrauer is trying to kill me."

"I would be concerned about that too," said Steven. "Do you check the uneven bars every time you get up there? It would all look like an accident . . ."

I let out a small moan, remembering my frustration as Ms. Bomtrauer made me try the impossible moves again and again and again while the sleeker, better-coordinated girls looked on.

"Poor Bethy," Noe cooed.

"It's okay," I said, letting myself be hugged, letting the familiar ocean of Noe restore me. The bad moment throbbed and ebbed and faded away, like a headache successfully quashed by a tab of aspirin.

We walked across the parking lot together, our jackets zipped up against the cold.

"If we do find your dead body squashed beneath a floor mat, we'll know who did it," Steven said.

35

THANKSGIVING WAS DUMB, AS ALWAYS. Noe
went to her grandparents' place, then joined Steven at some
fancy ski resort with his family. She called me gushing about
all the intense conversations she and Steven had been having,
and about the breakfast room at the ski lodge where you could
pour your own espresso shots from a machine. I went tobog-
ganing with my cousin Max and his friends and hung around
the house feeling bored.

"You should call Carly Ocean one of these days," Mom said
on Saturday morning, patting my hand.

As if I would go crawling to dumpy, pious Carly Ocean from
my old elementary school, Carly Ocean who I never wanted to

hang out with, ever, but who called me every break, persistent as a bloodhound.

"Carly Ocean's not my friend," I said.

But that same afternoon, Carly called and Mom guilted me into hanging out with her. We went to this stupid place for hot chocolate, and Carly gave me a pair of sparkly socks with a candy cane taped to the wrapping paper, as if we were still in fourth grade. Afterward, Carly wanted to go to a teen dance at the Lions Club. We picked up her friend Renata, a short girl with her hair in tiny braids. Carly and Renata went to the Catholic high school, St. Barnabas. Everything about Carly was pale and dull and slow. In my head, I could hear Noe saying, *What a cow.* When we got to the dance, there were some kids smoking a joint in the parking lot, and Carly and Renata made this wide circle to avoid walking near them.

"Well, *that's* illegal," Carly huffed.

I had a mean desire to tell her about Oliver just to see the look on her face, but I knew she'd tell her mom, and it wasn't worth the trouble.

I tried to dance with them, but I couldn't stand it. Carly smelled like eggs. She and her friend kept talking about the little kids they babysat, or asking me questions like was it true that a bunch of kids from E. O. James had gotten caught doing E, and acting like they felt sorry for me that I went to such a "bad" school.

I couldn't stand Carly's eggy sweat and Renata's braying giggle. They were asking me about boys at E. O. James when I spotted two of my coworkers from the ice-cream shop, Billie and Phinnea, across the gym. I left Carly and Renata behind and caught up with them.

"Hey, girl," shouted Phinnea over the music. "You look hot."

They pulled me into their crowd. It was a bunch of kids who work in the parks. I danced with them, and went to the bathroom with them to drink some flavored vodka that Billie had brought and take photos of the three of us on Phinnea's pink cell phone.

"Ice-cream girlzzzzz," said Billie, and the cell phone made a picture-taking sound. We drank another sip of vodka and Billie adjusted the pads in her bra. We went back out, and danced some more, and lip-synched along with the songs. We did silly dances and shouted ourselves hoarse.

Some of the SkyTram boys were there, and I ended up dancing with one of them. We shouted a few things at each other—name, school—but I couldn't really hear what the boy said and I don't think he heard me either.

Carly and Renata were somewhere, probably watching. The boy spun me around and our mouths met with a bump, more collision than kiss.

A panicky sorrow flapped in my chest. For some reason, I started thinking about the orchids nodding in the moonlight on the night of the homecoming dance, and the feeling of my bare feet in the spilled potting soil. I wanted to be there right now, in the quiet garden, or the forest. I hated the flashing lights and noise inside the dance. Why couldn't the whole world be like the wild place near the train tracks, soft and lush and humming? Why did everything people liked have to be so harsh and loud and plastic?

I broke away from the boy. "I have to go," I said.

I pushed into the crowd without waiting for his response. From the corner of my eye, I saw him cast about in confusion. *The forest*, I thought to myself. The only good place left was the forest. Why couldn't Noe love what I loved, for once? Why couldn't she see?

Renata found me in the bathroom. "Carly is crying because she's had really bad depression all year and she says you're her oldest friend."

I was ashamed. If I was the closest thing Carly had to a friend, her life had to be pretty dire. "I'll go find her," I mumbled.

I was friendly and attentive to Carly on the car ride home, but that almost made it worse. She sniffed and started telling me a long story about how all the boys at her school made fun of her because of how she smelled.

"They're just dumb," I said, but she *did* smell like eggs, and

I felt bad for lying and also hypocritical, because her eggy smell was part of what had driven me away.

"You got so skinny since we graduated from Wilson," Carly said.

"No, I didn't," I said.

Carly's beady eyes bored into me. "Margot Dilforth thinks you're anorexic. You and that gymnastics girl."

Margot Dilforth was one of the other kids from Wilson who went to E. O. James for high school. She'd always been a conspiracy theorist, reporting with wide-eyed earnestness about the kids she was "sure" were fighting or smoking pot or breaking up with one another.

"Oh, really," I said, rolling my eyes.

"Margot says she caught her throwing up in the bathroom."

"Uh-huh."

I didn't know why I was acting like that, all superior. Margot probably *had* caught Noe in one of her emergency purges. It was true, I thought to myself, but not in the way Carly thought. Noe was different. Noe was Noe. *Bulimics eat an entire chocolate cake and puke it up. I'm just trying to get this dead animal out of my body, if that's okay with you.* Even after all the messiness with our roommate plans, it still felt good to defend Noe, to be Annabeth, fiercely loyal one, the friend who understood.

"You *did* get skinnier," Carly said.

I was grateful, for the ten thousandth time that night, that I didn't have to see Carly Ocean more than once or twice a year.

At home, I went straight to my room. My school photo from a couple of years ago caught my eye. Annabeth in eighth grade. Carly was right. My face was rounder then. I stared at the photo. I tapped my finger against it, as if the eighth-grade Annabeth were trapped in there and could come back out.

Something began to ache inside me. I felt bad for the eighth-grade Annabeth. If she knew what was coming, she would have stayed in that photo forever.

My phone buzzed. Text from Phinnea.

u ok? bryan rlly likes you, and he's all worried that you left because you were mad at him.

I explained about Carly Ocean. my friend was crying, i had to go.

The texting wore me out. I turned off my phone. Mom knocked on my door in her pajamas, all "How was the dance?" I tipped the eighth-grade photo down before she noticed it.

"Just shoot me," I said.

I WAS GRATEFUL WHEN SCHOOL STARTED again.
Even though the break was only four days long, it felt like forever. I'd gotten a cold the day after the dance and spent Sunday
on the couch watching *Fraggle Rock*. I wasn't too sick to go
back to school, but I was still a little queasy and tired.

Noe had come back from the ski lodge wearing a brand-
new coat with a fake fur collar. At our lockers that morning,
she chattered about Darla. "She's like a second mom to me, you
know?"

Noe's mom was perfectly nice: generous and exhausted,
always making sure you had a drink and a snack. Noe couldn't
stand her.

"Why do you need a second mom?" I said, which seemed to make Noe annoyed.

That afternoon, we had a gym meet, the first one that counted for points. Noe got three first-place ribbons. My whole body felt heavy and I was sneezing so much I almost fell off the uneven bars, so for the rest of the afternoon I sat on the bleachers reading *How to Survive in the Woods*, two warm sweaters pulled over my leotard, a small mountain of tissues piling up beside me.

"Did you make out with Bryan Drexel?" Noe asked me on the bus ride home. "Rhiannon heard you did."

"Extenuating circumstances," I croaked. "You had to be there."

"You're getting to be so scandalous," Noe said. "You never even used to talk about boys, and suddenly you're the one-night-stand queen."

"I don't think a kiss counts as a one-night stand," I said.

"Darla thinks you're acting out your father issues," Noe said.

"What does Steven's mom know about my *father issues*?"

"Just because your dad left your mom doesn't mean that any boy you actually like is going to leave you."

"Noe. I was bored. I made out with Bryan Drexel. You don't have to come up with some big *interpretation*."

The bus jolted over a pothole, and I felt a wave of fatigue. I couldn't wait to get home and lie down. "In other news," I said, "Margot Dilforth has been telling people you throw up in the bathrooms."

Noe made a gesture of contempt encompassing the bus, the scenery, and the universe at large. She put her arm around my shoulder as if to assert our solidarity against the meddling Margot Dilforths of the world. "Margot Dilforth is an idiot," she said.

37

THE FIRST FRIDAY BACK FROM Thanksgiving, they herded all the seniors into the auditorium to drill us on the rules for campus visits. No drinking. No illegal substances. No sexual escapades. Noe and Steven held hands throughout the entire presentation, making plans to video chat every night of the three-day separation.

I wasn't quite so gung ho.

Uncle Dylan had called Ava to say I was coming and bought my Greyhound tickets online to get the early-bird price. Mom called her best friend, Pauline, who lives in the same town, to arrange for me to go over for dinner on my last night.

The town, Maple Bay, was an eight-hour bus ride away.

"We'll see each other all the time," Noe had reassured me when I'd expressed my dismay a second time. "You'll still come home for Christmas and stuff. Don't worry."

I stared at the map on my computer screen, with the route snaking across it in blue. I turned off my computer and lay on my bed with *How to Survive in the Woods*, but the route stayed pinned to the back of my eyes.

I had never been that far from home before.

38

THE MORNING BEFORE I WAS SUPPOSED to leave, I threw up in the garbage can next to my bed. I stared at the throw-up numbly, my body filling up with a terrible fore-knowledge.

Not possible, I thought. *So not possible.*

But my body clenched and rumbled and I threw up again.

I sat on my bed, my body curiously rigid, curiously light.

No, I thought to myself, *no, no, no, no.*

I listed all the reasons it couldn't be true: I was taking exactly half my pills, and Noe had said that was enough. The condom we'd used had mostly stayed on. I was underweight— the nutritionist had said so. Skinny girls couldn't get pregnant.

I tried to remember when I'd had my last period, but before the Pill I got it only every three or four months, and I wasn't sure when it was supposed to happen now that I was taking it.

Mom had left for work half an hour ago. I went downstairs, threw on my coat, and fired up the Honda, which I'd barely driven since my last shift at the ice-cream shop. The familiar houses jerked by, and the dented newspaper boxes that had melted snow pooled inside them, and the convenience store with wet bundles of firewood stacked beside the door. It seemed disloyal of the world to change like that, to be cold and dismal where it had been bright and scented and thrumming three months before. *Change back*, I wanted to scream. *Change back*. As if the winter was a cruel withholding by a universe that could just as easily churn out spring.

The drugstore was practically empty at that time of day, just a scattering of old men looking at vitamins and tired moms trying to resist their children's efforts at grabbing Christmas candy. *There's no reason to panic*, I told myself. *Any sane person wouldn't even bother with a test. I'm being paranoid.*

I found the tests in aisle 7 and put one in my basket, then covered it with a box of tampons and a pack of hair elastics and a chocolate Santa. The checkout clerk probably wouldn't even notice what I was buying, I told myself. They scanned so many barcodes it had to become automatic. Still, I was sweating under my snow coat. I didn't trust myself not to fumble the

PIN on the debit card reader, so I thrust a twenty-dollar bill at the cashier and did not meet her eyes while she counted the change into my hand.

At home, in the bathroom, a plus sign appeared. I wrapped the test up calmly, neatly, as one would in case of fire, and slid it to the bottom of the trash. I walked back to my bedroom and sat on my bed.

Outside, the last of the leaves on the birch tree were detaching themselves and spiraling down, detaching and spiraling down, landing on the snow-covered lawn. I watched them fall one by one, observing where they landed, as if I would be called to give an account of them later. When it got too windy to watch the leaves anymore, I put on *The Velvet Undergound* and listened to the entire album three times.

Finally, there was nothing to do but leave the house, so that is what I did.

IN THE "UNEXPECTED PREGNANCY" EPISODE of the TV series, the girl in trouble always Considers Her Options and Struggles with the Decision. She changes her mind a bunch and later, always wonders if she Did the Right Thing.

I was not a girl in a TV show. I'd made my decision in the seconds it took me to throw up in a garbage can. There was no going back and forth. No waiting for the decision to appear like a package in the mail. It just landed there, *thud*.

It was strange to be so certain.

You were supposed to agonize.

What did it mean that I wasn't agonizing?

In the TV show, the girl in trouble cried on her bed.

I listened to *The Velvet Underground* and walked in the forest.

I was more visibly upset the time I was eight and found a tick on my arm when I pulled off my sweater after one of our hikes—*Get it off me, get it off me!*—while Mom calmly went for the matches and tweezers.

Maybe it was her example that made me so certain, and so calm. Tick in jar. Tweezers in drawer. Then back to cooking the soup and chopping the wood, one cord for our fireplace and one for Nan's.

Isn't this what you secretly wanted? said a mean voice in my head. *An excuse to stay at home forever and never leave?*

Noe would want to be its auntie, I knew. She would coo and fuss and make lists of names in her day planner. In tenth grade, when Amanda Robinson got pregnant with Billy Shearer, Noe went nuts. She'd never even liked Amanda, but suddenly it was *Amanda and Billy* this, *Amanda and Billy* that, as if they were TV celebrities instead of Red Bull–swilling fifteen-year-olds who'd been dating for only three months. I'd seen Amanda and Billy around town, arguing in the Burger King parking lot while their baby wailed in its enormous plastic carrier. It didn't seem romantic to me. It seemed like the end of the world.

The woods were quiet. In my head, I was taking a magic pill that would make it go away. I was shaving my moustache. I was anywhere but here.

AFTER THE FOREST I DROVE DOWNTOWN. It looked smaller in the snow, and drearier. Raccoons rummaged in the ditches where garbage cans had overflowed. Buses sloshed up and down the street.

I saw on a bench in front of a gift shop.

A family with four kids wandered past me. The kids had those huge lollipops they sell to tourists, the kind you only ever see in cartoons. They had just unwrapped their lollipops and were trying to figure out the best strategy for consuming them. The thing is, though, it's impossible to get your mouth around them, and if you just lick the surface you can't get the full flavor. I watched the kids bringing the lollipops to their faces at different angles, realizing the dimensions were all wrong to get a good lick, looking confused but still determined, as if they couldn't believe that these enormous pink and blue things that looked so tantalizing were basically impossible to enjoy. You have to smash them into pieces to be able to suck on them at all, but kids are never willing to do that. Besides, once you do break off a piece, you realize how bad and headachey it tastes, and you don't want to eat it anymore.

When I got too cold from sitting, I went to the Unbelievable! Museum.

The museum is in a white house, with a white painted sign out front, and a replica of a barrel that someone had used to go over the waterfall in the 1920s. You can climb into the barrel and have your picture taken with your head sticking out the top. I have six or seven pictures of myself in this barrel at different ages, always grinning, my face bright with schemes to build a barrel of my own. The barrel is made of thick planks of wood encased in rings of steel. It swallows you up. It feels unbreakable. You can imagine cozying up inside it with a blanket and a book, and never noticing the roaring, rushing tumble over the waterfall.

Inside the museum, there's a goat with two heads and a wax figure of a woman with six fingers on both hands, as well as her delicate pink six-fingered gloves with pearl buttons up the side. There's a rat king, which is when a nest of rats gets their tails tangled up in a knot and can't get untangled again. They die like that, a writhing mass of rats, and eventually get discovered and stuck in curiosity museums. But the strangest thing in the collection is the lithopedion.

At first it looks like a fossil or rock; not a big deal compared to a two-headed goat. But if you read the typed yellow card, you discover that it is actually a rock-baby retrieved from the stomach of a seventy-year-old woman. Lithopedions are exceptionally rare. They happen when a baby starts to grow in the wrong place, and the body builds a shield of calcium around it. Medieval records of lithopedions tell stories of women who knew they were pregnant but "the baby never came out," and eventually they forgot about it and went on with their lives.

Maybe, I thought to myself, if I was lucky, the same thing would happen to me. My body would quietly digest the bundle of cells inside it, or it would fossilize them and turn them to stone. In fifty years, I would feel a pain in my stomach, and doctors would extract a pebble the size of aquarium gravel.

Do you know what this is, ma'am? they would say, holding it up with tweezers, and I would shake my head in bewilderment. *No, I have no idea.*

"The museum is closing," said the girl at the counter.

I took my winter jacket from the coat hook and walked out.

I DIDN'T FEEL LIKE GOING HOME.

I drove past the Java Bean where kids from my school were eating maple donuts, and the No Frills where Mom was working. The McDonald's PlayPlace looked like a strange tumor growing out of the side of the building. It snaked around bulbously while little kids clambered around inside it.

I drove past the go-kart track where my cousin Max works in the summer, and the K-Mart with the French fry truck outside.

Finally I went to the Botanical Gardens and parked in the empty lot.

The Botanical Gardens stay open year-round, although

there are no flowers in winter. You can walk around the frozen grounds, gazing at the red berries on the winter trees and the topiary unicorn glittering with frost. The ice-cream shop is closed but Jeanette Fielding is still in her office, filling out order forms for next year's Dixie cups and waffle cones.

The orchid house was empty. Not a single purple face to peep at, no nodding pink things on stems.

I remembered the first time Mom took me to the Gardens. How we spent all afternoon singing to the ducks in the pond and talking to flowers. How dizzy sweet the cosmos, how giggling and jesterly the jacaranda. How the whole garden became a many-tendriled friend I swam through under the sunshine.

Cold air was blowing through the broken pane of greenhouse glass.

I sat on the ground and took out my phone.

I supposed I had better tell Oliver.

I CALLED OLIVER'S NUMBER. THE GIRL who answered sang, "This is Loreen, Alaskan booty queen."

If it wasn't my life, I would have laughed.

43

LOREEN, ALASKAN BOOTY QUEEN, SOUNDED drunk.

"I need to talk to Oliver," I said.

"Who's this?" she drawled suspiciously.

I paused, but couldn't think of anything that rhymed with my name. "This is Annabeth, ice cream girl from hell. I need to speak to Oliver *now*."

Loreen didn't like the sound of that.

"Why?" she said. "What's your business?"

"Pregnancy."

She said she'd get him straightaway.

WHEN OLIVER CAME ON THE PHONE he was drunk too. It was noisy in the background: thrashing rock music and a sports game on TV. I wondered where he was. It was too early in the day for a bar, and Oliver was underage. Maybe Alaska was just loud.

"Annabeth," he shouted into the phone. "Hey-hey."

"Hey-hey," I echoed back.

"Whuss going on?"

Was there a snowstorm over there? Sound of howling winds and rattling flagpoles. Maybe he was on the crab boat, although I didn't see how that was possible cell service–wise, or how Loreen, Alaskan Booty Queen, fit into the picture. Maybe she was the skipper.

"I'm pregnant," I said.

"No you're not."

"Is she pregnant?" A screech from Loreen.

And Oliver: "It's just some chick from home starting drama."

Loreen: "Are you lying to me?"

Oliver: "Loreen!"

Slamming door. A roar from the TV. Someone must have scored a touchdown.

A few seconds later, Oliver came back on the phone.

"That was real uncool, Annabeth," he said. "We barely hung out and I've been gone for two months. You can't call me up and get all pissed that I'm with another girl. Now she thinks I knocked you up."

"You did."

"We used protection."

"Not the whole time."

Horrified silence. Terrifying possibilities invoked.

"Oliver?" I said. "Oliver."

On TV, the cheering continued. They must be passing out free burritos in the stadium, dropping them out of a plane. Oliver stayed quiet for so long I thought he had passed out. I was about to hang up when he spoke suddenly.

"You can do whatever you want," Oliver said, "but I'm not coming back."

I kicked an empty flowerpot with my snow boot. "I'm not

asking you to come back."

"Then why'd you call?"

It was my turn to go silent. The words dropped out of my grasp like an armful of library books. Why *had* I called? Why had I gone to the forest and the curiosity museum? Why had I done any of the things I had done that strange, cold day?

"I just thought you would want to know," I stammered, and hung up the phone.

THE ORCHID HOUSE WAS A KNOT of silence in the middle of a silent garden. It glittered like a broken Christmas ornament in the snow.

I walked across the frozen grass toward the rose garden, not really sure what I was doing. It was getting dark; time to go home. Time to figure out the next thing to do. I pulled my coat around me tight and stuffed my hands deep in the pockets to warm them up. I wished I hadn't told Oliver. I didn't even know why I had. I guess I thought you were supposed to, but maybe that was an idea from a TV show.

As I walked around the garden, I pretended I was an explorer on an alien planet. The rosebushes were black and frostbitten, spiky, thorny things in cold beds of dirt. The wedding gazebo was a docking pad for a flying saucer. I came to the duck pond and threw a rock at the ice. It didn't shatter; it didn't even make a dent.

I was acting all wrong. Like a mental patient, or a little kid. Maybe I lacked some kind of basic human instinct. Maybe I'd inherited that from him.

I stuffed some snow in my mouth to numb the thought.

"Annabeth," called a voice from across the pond.

I looked up and saw a fat man with a dog. The dog was snuffling at the snow, digging up a long-lost waffle cone someone had dropped there at the end of summer. The man waved a mittened hand and came lumbering toward me, the dog tugging at its leash behind him. Close up, I recognized him as the nutritionist.

"Hey, Bob," I said. "What are you doing here?"

"Just walking String Bean. What about you?"

"Just thinking about stuff," I said.

He had earbuds dangling out the collar of his coat. In the quiet of the garden, I could hear the tinny voice talking out of them. *Kingdom of Stones.*

"My grandmother used to say if you eat snow, you'll freeze your insides," said the nutritionist. He looked jolly in the snow, with his dog at his feet. Fresher and happier. Maybe "jolly" is an insulting way of putting it, but I mean it in the best possible way.

"My grandma thinks the chemicals in snow give you cancer," I said.

"I certainly hope not," said Bob. String Bean tugged at his leash. I reached down and petted him. "So, how are things going?" said Bob.

"Good."

"Enjoying gymnastics?"

"Sort of. I mostly signed up for my friend."

"I talked to the cafeteria manager about serving more vegetarian food."

"Oh yeah?"

"I'm supposed to give them a list of meal requests. If you want to drop by sometime and help me come up with some ideas, it would be a big help. Otherwise it's going to be rice and beans. And snow for dessert."

"Okay," I said.

String Bean barked at a bird. The narrator of *Kingdom of Stones* was talking about a pond in which Rae the Stone Maiden had been frozen by a wizard.

"You probably don't want to miss this part," I said, gesturing at Bob's earbuds. "I need to get going anyway."

Bob nodded and wrapped String Bean's leash around his hand. "Nice to run into you, Annabeth."

"See ya later, Bob."

I felt lighter walking back to my car and I didn't know why. Maybe I just needed someone to remind me that in a few days, once this was taken care of, life was going to go on as normal. There was going to be cafeteria food and Noe's half-annoying, half-lovable chatter during gymnastics practice. I wasn't a freak or a monster, just a kid who wasn't careful enough. I certainly wasn't any worse than Oliver.

I got into the cold car and turned the heat all the way up.

In the TV show, the girl in trouble parks by the waterfall and calls her best friend.

I left my phone on the seat and walked to the damp iron railing alone.

Birds were swooping back and forth in front of the colored floodlights they shine on the waterfall at night. I watched them soar and circle, their wings stained pink and green by the light.

I stayed until my hands were frozen and my eyelashes wet with snow. Until I could feel the waterfall inside my skull, and the rocks it crashed against, and there was nothing left to do but go back home.

IF YOU COME TO MY TOWN in the winter, you will
inevitably end up at the waterfall at night. You will watch those
same birds swooping. Maybe you will stare at the water that
rushes over the edge and hear the roaring gushing and feel the
chill of mist on your skin.

Maybe you will feel, for the first or the thousandth time,
how many things in the world are bigger than you.

WHEN MOM CAME HOME FROM WORK, she buzzed around the house, all *I can't believe my baby is going to Maple Bay for three days*. You would think I was going on a mission to Mars in the morning, the way she beamed and babbled.

We made dinner together, and Mom helped me pack sweaters, jeans, a scarf, a hat, and presents for Ava and Pauline.

"You're going to have so much fun with Ava. She's changed so much since she went away. Maybe she can give you some advice about which classes to take."

She plucked a pair of socks out of my dresser and stuffed it cheerfully into my bag.

I almost told her then, but I didn't.

WHEN MOM WENT TO BED, I walked to the end of our block and called Ava.

It was snowing. Flakes landed on my nose while I waited for her to pick up.

She owed me a favor, I thought to myself. If it came down to it, I could blackmail her into taking me. If Mom or Nan or Uncle Dylan found out that Ava had told me about my dad, they would never forgive her, even though she was crazy when she did it. Even though the first thing she did when she stopped being crazy was write me a letter apologizing, a letter I still had buried in my dresser drawer.

The phone rang and rang. *Nine weeks*, I thought to myself.

The internet said nine weeks was an okay time to do it. At least I wasn't too late. At least I wasn't in denial for months, like Mom was, or paralyzed by distress. At least I had Ava to call, and money from my ice-cream job, and a bus ticket to a town far away. I was better off than a lot of people. There were so many ways it could have been worse.

In case of emergency, says Wilda McClure in *How to Survive in the Woods*, *enumerate your advantages*.

I stood in the snow and enumerated, and on the eighth ring Ava picked up the phone.

49

"HEY, LADY," SHE SAID.

I swallowed hard. "Hey," I said.

"Are you still coming tomorrow?"

Her voice was cheerful. It was hard to get used to the new Ava. Sometimes the change still startled me. *I went through a real shitty time in high school and I'm sorry I inflicted that shittiness on you,* she'd written in her letter. *I think in some ways I was jealous because everyone loved you so much, and I felt like I came second to you and Max. I'm sorry about your dad and sorry you had to find out in such a horrible way. If you ever want to talk about it, I'm here, even though I understand if you don't like me very much anymore.*

I shivered. The truth was, I never wanted to talk about it. Not with Mom, not with Ava, not with anyone. It was too disgusting. It made my skin creep. And even though Ava had taken back some of the terrible things she had said, in my worst moments I still felt like an interloper.

Ava was waiting for me to answer.

My voice trembled. "Yeah."

Snowflakes were falling around me in dense flurries. The houses on the street were quiet and dark.

"What's wrong?" Ava said.

I didn't answer.

"Annabeth," she said more sternly, "what's wrong?"

"I need a favor," I said.

50

THE NEXT DAY, MOM DROVE ME to the Greyhound
station to catch the bus to Maple Bay. It had snowed all night,
and the fire hydrants wore fat white hats. Parked cars had
sheets of snow draped over their windshields. They looked like
hospital patients.

"Did you remember your toothbrush?" Mom said. She
acted happy on the drive, but I could tell she was as nervous
as I was. She hugged me and I tensed involuntarily, afraid she
would detect my still-undetectable condition through both our
snow coats.

"Give Pauline a hug for me," said Mom. "Ava too."

"I will."

She gave me a twenty-dollar bill for no apparent reason and kissed me on the cheek. "Love you, Annabean. Have fun up there."

"Love you too."

51

THE BUS RIDE TO MAPLE BAY had a million stops. Every bus station had the same crumbly look as all the others, a concrete lip where people waited with their overstuffed bags, dirty yellow lights. Every highway exit had the same fast-food restaurants and gas stations. I slumped against the window and tried to pick out a tree or plant, some green thing my heart could curl its tendrils around and try to befriend. Why had we done this? I thought to myself. If nobody loved it, why? It was insane to build places that nobody loved. It was insane to cover all that was green and tender with parking lots and garbage bins.

I wondered if anyone else felt that way, or if I was just a freak. As the bus huffed and belched and pulled back onto the highway, a loneliness overcame me that was worse than anything I'd felt all year.

Midway through the morning, Noe texted me.

are you still mad at me?

i didn't realize you thought i was promising to go with you.

i thought we were just talking and having fun.

It was so like Noe to wait until a time when we wouldn't see each other for several days to start a dialogue like this.

i don't know, I texted back.

it was the way you came back from the gym expo

and didn't even bother to talk to me

like i should just adapt to your plans

A few seconds later, a string of texts from Noe came back.

i don't want you to adapt to my plans

you should always do what you want, k?

you're so incredible and smart

you don't need me to tell you what to do

I stared at my phone. I didn't have the energy to contradict her or call out all the truths she wasn't acknowledging. It was easier to snuggle into the familiar ritual of flattery and reconciliation; easier to be lovable Annabeth, pliant and understanding, than to let out a more disruptive version of myself. I thought of the sunny afternoon when I told her about Oliver, and tears pricked at my eyes.

i know, I typed back.

i just got scared

i don't want to lose you

you won't lose me

we'll visit all the time

i'll come stay in your dorm room

and you'll come home on breaks

:)

steven says you're fascinating, btw

we talked about you for like an hour

aww

he was all, "she's an undercover badass!"

and i was like, "i know!"

you guys are the best

oh

bus is stopping

have to pee

talk soon

talk soon

In a McDonald's bathroom noisy with flushing toilets and keening hand dryers, I splashed cold water on my face, shook out my stale ponytail, finger-combed my hair. Beside me, enterprising women were brushing their teeth, putting on lipstick, taking swipes at their armpits with deodorant sticks.

"You done with the sink?" a woman said, elbowing in beside me and planting her enormous purse on the water-spotted countertop.

"Yeah, sorry," I stuttered. I wished I could feel as confident as her. Swing my purse around. Take out a can of perfume and spray it at myself with such gusto that anyone in a six-foot blast radius must duck or be scented with Eau de Sex Sugar.

I trudged back to the empty bus, climbed on, and rummaged in the overhead bin for *How to Survive*. The seats with their detritus of squashed sweaters and half-drunk soda bottles looked like the little shrines people make at gravestones; plastic flowers gone crooked and leaky from wind and rain.

Our next rest stop had a mini grocery. I circled around the aisles, picking things up, inspecting them, and mentally disqualifying them. Everything was too expensive: two dollars for a flimsy little Oats 'n Honey bar that wouldn't fill me up, a dollar twenty-five for a waxy, red, poisonous-looking apple, three dollars for something called a Yogurt Parfait, which was a plastic cup with white stuff at the bottom, then purplish jelly, then some oaty stuff that was supposed to be granola but surely couldn't be. I could hear Noe's voice inside my head, reading the ingredients lists out loud. *Gelatin, delicious. Chocolate milk? You might as well drink a cup of corn syrup.*

I circled for ten minutes, deliberating, half swooning under the too-bright fluorescent lights. All around me, people were grabbing things off the racks and buying them, filling paper cups with soft drinks from the machines against one wall, retrieving sunburned-looking hot dogs from the heated glass display case on the counter. I had that terrible feeling like in musical chairs, when the music stops and everyone else has gone for their chair and you run around the circle in a panic and you *just can't find one.*

Finally I spied some discount cinnamon rolls, on special two for ninety-nine cents.

Two cinnamon rolls for ninety-nine cents. It sounded pretty Special to me. It wouldn't pass the Noe test, but I was getting desperate. I took them back to the bus and ate them one after the other, unpeeling the sticky spirals until I got to the nutty place at the middle. When I was finished my hands were covered in sugar goo. I crumpled up the plastic wrap they had come in and tucked it into the seat pocket in front of me. The bus rumbled and bounced over the highway. A few minutes later I was not feeling good.

"Excuse me," I said to the woman sitting next to me. "I have to get out."

She grunted and moved her legs grudgingly. I clambered over them and staggered down the aisle to the very back of the bus, where there was a tiny bathroom. Before the flimsy door shut behind me, two very Special cinnamon buns had curdled into poison inside me.

I am a skinny person. There is not room in my stomach for so much burning slop. But still it came surging up my throat, *retch retch retch*, until I was dizzy, seeing spots, and had to grab at the grubby stall walls for balance.

I rinsed my mouth at the dirty sink. I was pretty sure the whole bus had heard me heaving. Back in my row, the woman who was sitting next to me had changed seats—so much the better.

I sat down carefully and took a sip of water from the bottle Mom had made me bring. I felt so nauseous from the shuddering and the cinnamon buns and from the thought, urgent and terrifying, that things at the clinic would not work out (the river would rise! the horse would stumble! a log would fall across the road!) and I would be stuck with a drooling, screaming Oliver-baby I did not want and could not love. I stuck my earbuds into my ears and played *The Velvet Underground*, but I kept thinking about everything that could go wrong.

I must have looked like I was crying or something. An old woman bundled up in a bright pink snowsuit moved herself across the aisle to sit beside me.

"Where are you headed, honey?"

I grappled with the earbuds, collected myself, and smiled at her. "Maple Bay."

"Is that home?"

I shook my head. "I'm supposed to go on a tour of Northern University."

"You look too young to be going to university."

"I'm seventeen."

"Where's home for you?"

I named my town.

"Oh, I love it there. The Botanical Gardens."

The old lady had violet eye shadow and violet nail polish to match. I imagined her house. It would have an upright piano and a basket full of magazines and a mischievous poodle that barked at the mailman.

"You've been to the Gardens?" I said. "I work at the ice-cream shop in the summer."

"You do?" she said. "How lovely."

The bus rolled over a pothole. I felt my throat rise, and made a grab for the paper barf bag in the seat pocket. The old lady patted my shoulder sympathetically.

"Was that you throwing up in the bathroom?" she said.

I cringed. "Sorry," I said. "I know it's gross."

"Would you like a ginger pill? I get sick on buses too."

She dug a small bottle out of her purse and held it out to me. I shook my head. "It won't help."

"It's good for all kinds of motion sickness."

"It's not that kind of sickness," I said. "It'll be over soon."

I don't know why I said it like that, so obvious. I guess I was hoping the old lady would turn out to be a magic spirit friend who would give me wise advice and send me off with a talisman, an eagle feather or a mantra to repeat in my darkest hour. *Everyone deserves a second chance, honey cakes. Be strong.*

Rumble rumble rumble, went the bus. The old lady dug in

her purse again and pulled out a religious tract. In a high, quavering voice she began to read out loud.

"Lord, drive out the forces of Satan—"

I popped up from my seat, grabbed my backpack, and fled to the back of the bus.

"Was that old lady reading Scripture at you?" said the heavily mascaraed twentysomething girl I wedged myself next to. She was wearing a ripped black T-shirt and had a backpack shaped like a teddy bear.

I nodded.

She popped her gum. "Crazy bitch."

52

THERE WERE TREES OUTSIDE THE WINDOW now. I wondered when that had happened. They were standing thick and dense on either side of the road. The bus began to climb a hill, and suddenly the trees dropped away to reveal a view of low mountains with forests stretching as far as I could see. My breath stopped, and I craned my neck to see better, as if I could get closer to that view, climb into it and have it belong to me.

So this is what Mom was talking about, I thought. This is what she wanted me to feel. A tug of belonging. A sense of the infinite.

I put my head against the window and sobbed.

WHEN THE BUS GOT INTO MAPLE Bay, Ava was waiting for me at the station. She was wearing a green velvet coat and an orange knitted cap. Her hair was dyed blue and her eyes were their regular color. When I walked up to her with my bag, she pulled me into a hug whose ferocity surprised me.

"Your mom is going to kill me," she said.

54

AVA'S DORM WAS ACTUALLY AN OLD brick house on the west side of campus. It had six bedrooms, a kitchen, and a wood-paneled study room like the library in *Clue*. The kitchen had a bookshelf built into the wall. I looked at the books while Ava made tea. *The Complete Works of Shakespeare, Waiting for Godot, 50 Short Plays, The Actor Prepares*. I watched the self-assured way Ava moved around the kitchen, pawing through the cupboard for clean mugs and retrieving a crusty jar of honey from some hiding place under the counter.

"Besides certain dickheads in Alaska," said Ava, "how's life?"

"Fine," I said. "Mom's good. Nan's good. I'm on the gymnastics team."

Even though Ava had reformed, I still felt shy around her. The fact that she was a Good Witch now instead of a Bad Witch hardly mattered; any way you sliced it, change was still uncomfortable.

"Where's your friend?" said Ava. "When I saw you in the summer, your mom said you guys were planning to drive up here together."

"She's touring Gailer College."

Ava made an *I knew it* face. "She seemed like the Gailer type."

I'd forgotten that Ava had met Noe briefly, at my house. "I'm applying there too," I said stoutly, as if to defend Noe from whatever *the Gailer type* implied. "Everybody is. The only reason I even came up here was because Mom made me."

It was weird to see Ava so bright and capable. Uncle Dylan was right. She'd really come into her own at Northern. The darkness that had been suffocating her before had dissipated, like a plant that only seemed to be dying until you shook out its roots and planted it in a deeper hole. Ava didn't come back to our town much anymore, even for Christmases and Thanksgivings. The avoidance was definitely intentional. Some people fought tooth and nail to keep their old life alive when they went away, but as far as I knew Ava never talked to her high school friends, never came home on college breaks to work her old summer job and go to parties with people she'd known since she was a kid.

I couldn't tell if it was better to be a person who held on or a person who let go. Maybe it was less about better and worse, and more about which thing you needed to do in order for your plant to grow.

Ava handed me a chipped mug that was shaped like a mushroom. It had some green flecks inside it that must be the tea. Before that, I'd only ever had Lipton tea in bags with a string and a tag. When I sipped the mushroom mug, the green flecks stuck to my teeth.

"I don't know what I would have done if I hadn't gotten out of there," Ava said. "Probably killed myself."

"Why?"

"Sit by the railroad tracks one day and think about it," Ava said.

I had spent plenty of days by the railroad tracks.

I didn't know what she was talking about.

The grass there is bleached to pale white straw, and crickets jump past your legs like popcorn kernels zinging off a hot pan. When the trains come by they huff and chug and clang your brain to noisy oblivion. Afterward you can follow the tracks to a dusty grove where kids make jumps for their dirt bikes and hobos leave behind nests of broken glass.

"Mom and Nan and Uncle Dylan seem to like it okay," I said.

"They all left and went back. That's different. Your mom really wants you to come here," said Ava. "And you're Nature Girl. Come on. There're a million acres of national park fifteen minutes away."

Are you a Noe? she seemed to be saying, *or an Ava? Are you going to hold on to what you already have, or start from scratch?*

I gazed into my mug. The green flecks were swirling around in the tea like the snow inside a snow globe.

"I just don't know yet," I said, and set it down.

I WAS HOPING AVA AND I would go to bed right away so we wouldn't have to talk anymore, but Ava's roommates started bubbling in and soon it was impossible to escape.

Ava's roommates were different from anyone I knew from back home. I couldn't keep their names straight. Girls in thick glasses and tight sweaters and dresses rescued from the costume department thrift sale, they made tea and sat on the counter and picked at the runs in their stockings.

"What's your name?" they asked me.

"Annabeth."

"How old are you? Where do you live? I like your jeans. Aren't her jeans cute? Where did you get them? Did you drive up here alone? A bunch of us are going out for breakfast tomorrow morning, do you want to go out for breakfast?"

I kept hoping Ava would step in to save me like Noe always did when people were overwhelming me with too much attention, but she left me to answer for myself.

"I took the bus," I said, "I'm seventeen," feeling like the contestant in a rapid-fire trivia game.

"Were you on the eight o'clock?" said a girl with dreadlocks.

"Mm-hmm."

"My friend was on that bus, she said there was this girl who was crying and throwing up the whole way."

Heat flooded my face. If Noe were here, she'd be distracting Ava's roommates, telling them about vegetarianism or gymnastics. She'd be making plans for us to go to a physics lecture with one of them and a People for the Ethical Treatment of Animals meeting with another. I wouldn't have to talk at all except to peep my excitement or consent. This was why I couldn't go to Northern without her, exactly this: surrounded by strangers, my only ally a cousin who apparently refused to protect me.

"What's wrong?" said the girls. "What's wrong?"

I was doing my werewolf thing, my capacity for language disappearing, my ability to smile and present a functional social face melting away. *Where's Noe?* my inside self was howling. Already, my mind was frantically making plans. I would tell Mom I hated Northern, I would rip up the application I'd been working on, I would go to Gailer College and be the water girl for the gymnastics team and never leave Noe again.

Ava was gazing at me across the kitchen. She raised her eyebrows and tipped her head to the side as if to say, *What's going on in there?*

"Nothing," I squeaked at the girls who had asked me what was wrong. "The bus ride was shitty."

I looked at the floor. The roots of my plant were crying out in alarm and groping for familiar soil. I ordered myself to stay and talk, but my feet began to move without my consent and suddenly I was on the front steps of Ava's dorm, huddled up against a brick column. Through the kitchen window, I could hear Ava and her friends.

"Is she okay? She, like, *bolted.*"

"She's *really* shy. It's pretty much her first time away from home. I'll go out there in a minute if she doesn't come back in."

I took out my phone and called Noe, but she didn't answer. I remembered that tonight was the tiki party. Noe was probably dancing in a little group with all the other kids from our school, her phone crammed deep in her purse or forgotten on some bathroom counter.

There was a text from Mom I hadn't noticed before.

if you get this in time, take a picture for me when you go past moose rock!

I stared at the text for a moment, wondering what she was

talking about, then remembered that a bunch of people had taken pictures out the bus window when we passed a weirdly shaped boulder a few minutes from town. It was strange to think that Mom had spent a part of her life here, that she knew this place that I was just discovering. I thought about how excited I was when I'd first pulled *How to Survive in the Woods* out of our basement. Mom had made notes in the margins, blue ink additions to the diagrams of cooking shelters and proper canoe-paddling strokes. In the plant identification section, she'd marked a date and place next to each plant on the day that she first found it. Wild strawberries were marked *Maple Bay National Park* the summer before I was born.

Next year! she'd written next to a place on the map, a zig-zagging network of lakes and rivers.

Next year had never happened. Next year, she was back home.

As I sat on the steps, anger welled up inside me for the lost girl of the survival book, full of exclamation marks and opinions on the proper way to build a fire in the rain. She wanted so much for me to discover myself, and I was afraid to even try.

It was starting to snow. I texted Mom back quickly and stood up to go back inside.

56

WHEN I WENT BACK INTO THE kitchen, the girls were making cookies. The counter was littered with dirty spoons and mixing bowls, and half the contents of the cupboards were piled up on the table.

"Were you hiding?" said the girl with dreadlocks, whose name might have been Beatrice. "We didn't mean to scare you away."

"It's okay," I said. "I was just embarrassed."

"Awwww," said Beatrice. "So you were the puking girl. Are you feeling better now? What happened?"

I hesitated. How could I tell a bunch of strangers when I hadn't told Noe? Wasn't that a kind of betrayal? Maybe I was still angry at her for ditching our plans so easily, and this was my twisted way of getting back at her. Or maybe I trusted Ava's friends in a way I didn't trust Noe. They seemed so grown-up, and we were still kids. I needed a grown-up right now, not a kid—did that make me a traitor? I wasn't sure.

I thrust these complicated thoughts aside and blurted, "I had an accident. With a boy. Ava's taking me to the clinic tomorrow."

The kitchen was quiet for a moment. Then one by one, the girls put down their bowls and spatulas and teacups and came to put their hands on my shoulders and back.

"Are you scared?" they said.

"I don't know yet."

"Don't be scared!" they said. "Don't be scared!"

The girls all had some story about a close call they had had with a broken condom or a birth control pill.

"My twin sister tried to do an herbal abortion when we were fifteen," said a big, dark-haired girl who might have been called Jade or Jane or Jacey. "She got the recipe out of a fantasy novel. We stayed up all night brewing herbs on the stove." She chomped her cookie, then peered at it suspiciously. "How old was that butter?"

"Which book was it?" everyone wanted to know.

"That one with the fairies." She glanced at me appraisingly. "We could do one tomorrow, if you want. Co-op opens at eight, they have all the herbs."

"Keep your witchy paws off my baby cousin," said Ava.

"Annabeth, don't listen to her, she has no idea what she's talking about."

A girl named Leah started telling a story about a time she got pregnant by accident. "He was like, 'It broke and I don't have another one!' And I was like, 'Okaaaaay, I guess we have to stop.' And then we were like, 'What if we're really, really careful? Like, ninja-careful!'"

Leah had had an abortion at the same clinic I was going to in the morning.

"The people at the clinic are really nice," she said. "They're really nice. You're going to be okay."

Ava's roommates reminded me of a chorus of batty aunts in a musical, trading off solos in a medley of reassurance and advice. I couldn't believe they were only three years older than me and Noe and everyone in our year at school. They seemed so different, somehow. Like they belonged to a bigger world.

When Ava took out the last tray of cookies, everyone gathered around to gobble them up. I hung back, grateful for the distraction. When the cookies were gone, the girls had moved on from their cheerful interrogation and started talking among themselves.

At one a.m. Ava's roommates dumped the cookie trays in the sink without washing them and tromped up the stairs to bed.

"Tired?" Ava said.

I nodded.

"Come on. I'll show you my room."

57

IN THE MORNING, AVA TOOK ME to the clinic. The nurse asked me some questions and had me pee in a cup, and put me down for an appointment the following morning. They couldn't fit me in the same day. At first I was disappointed, then relieved. It meant I wouldn't have to miss the campus tour that Mom had signed me up for. Even though that was a small thing, it seemed important somehow—like at least I wouldn't have to let her down in that one regard. So when she asked me about Northern, I'd have something to tell her about.

Ava and I drove back to campus and she left me in the student union building to wait for my tour guide. I sat on a purple couch and took out *How to Survive in the Woods*. A few minutes later, a boy in a bright blue shirt with NORTHERN

UNIVERSITY on the front asked if I was Annabeth. He had geeky glasses and a hat with earflaps and a button that said NATIVE AMERICAN STUDENT CENTER.

"I love that book," he said, tapping the cover. "They sell it in the bookstore here. Did you know Wilda McClure's from Maple Bay?"

The boy's name was Loren, and he was in his first year, studying forestry.

"We can swing by her old house after the tour, if you want. It's a museum now. It's kind of cool."

First, we went to the Arts building and the Science building and the Engineering building and the Music building, and through the freshman dorms. Some people had their doors open. I peeked into the rooms as we walked down the hall, making a mental note to tell Noe that they already came with mini-fridges before I remembered that she wasn't applying. Loren told me about the dragon boat race that happened every April, and the community farm where students could grow their own vegetables and learn to milk a cow.

The Wilda McClure house had an exhibit on the ground floor with all her old camping stuff. Wilda McClure's tent. Wilda McClure's backpack. The binoculars and notebook with which Wilda McClure tracked the comings and goings of wolves. Loren caught me staring at the glass display case with the canoe and smooth wooden paddles in which Wilda McClure had explored over two hundred lakes.

"My mom would love this," I said. "It's actually her book."

"Want me to take a picture of you with the canoe?"

"Nah."

"Come on. You've got to have something to show the parents."

Loren grinned. I hesitated, then dug my phone out of my bag. "The camera's not very good."

I stood beside the canoe with my arms at my sides.

"Smile," Loren said.

While he was taking the picture, the museum attendant came out from behind her booth. "Now one of you together," she said.

It was weird to explain that we were complete strangers, so Loren gave her the phone and I moved over so he could stand beside me.

"Say cheese," said the museum attendant.

"Cheese," Loren and I said.

I texted the first picture to Mom while we were walking back to the student union building.

oh my god, is that the wilda mcclure house? she texted back.

It made my heart break a little to know that Mom was so excited for me.

campus tour was awesome, I typed. **going to lunch with ava, then theater lecture.**

amazing! Mom wrote. **have fun.**

THAT NIGHT WAS AVA'S ROOMMATE'S birthday. We
all ate cake and drank something called Moscow Mules in the
warm, messy kitchen, then bundled up in our hats and coats
and mittens and dragged some big pieces of cardboard to a
place called Half Moon Mountain, which was really more of
a steep, snowy hill at the far edge of campus that looked down
over the forest and town. You could slide down on the cardboard like a toboggan, with the twinkly lights of town rushing
at you and the dark, jagged trees whispering past on either side,
then tromp back up the hill on stairs someone had cut into the
snow.

I slid again and again, sometimes sitting on the cardboard,
sometimes Superman-style with my stomach bumping over

the snow, sometimes in a long chain with Ava and Ava's room-mates. The sound was all muffled out there. Like if you brushed away the tiny sprinkling of voices and laughter, you could hear the sound of the earth itself. The more I climbed and slid and screamed, the louder the earth seemed to speak, until I could feel its voice all around me.

Loren had said there was an outdoor program at Northern that was founded in honor of Wilda. You spent half the year "in the field," tracking wolves and taking tests of river water and learning about forest fires. Maybe I could do that. Maybe I could be another Wilda. As I hurtled down the hill on my sled, it didn't seem unthinkable anymore.

On the way back to the dorm, Ava borrowed my phone to tell another one of her friends where we were. "Who's the cutie?" she said, clicking the camera app shut to make the call.

"He's just the campus tour guy. The museum lady wanted to take a picture."

"Did you get his number?"

I blushed. "Ava. I'm not exactly looking."

She put an arm around my shoulder. "Oh, don't pull the fallen woman thing on me. That's such horseshit. You think guys feel the need to punish themselves for the heinous crime of *having a body*?"

"I need some time for myself."

"That's different. *Need some time*, okay. *Nobody can ever love me after this*, not okay. *I can't love myself after this*, not okay. Would you feel bad for meeting a cute boy if Oliver was the one having the appointment?"

"I don't know," I said.

She bopped me on the shoulder. "Think about it."

Ava was big on *think about it* these days.

We came to the dorm and went inside. While Ava was taking a shower, I took her laptop to the common room and curled up with it on a couch. Noe had uploaded a million pictures of the River Rats game and the tiki party, with Noe, Lindsay, Rhiannon, and Kaylee grinning in bright orange clothes. I'd come back from Half Moon Mountain in an expansive mood, but as I gazed at the screen my temples began to throb. There is something haunting about seeing pictures of your friends having a good time without you, even if you were having a good time in parallel, even if you were having the time of your life. Suddenly, you have one memory and your friend has another, and you'll never be able to say, *Remember that time?* and never laugh together, remembering. A part of me would rather have had a mediocre time at a River Rats game with Noe than a great time on Half Moon Mountain, because the River Rats game would have increased the space where the circles in our Venn diagram overlapped, and Half Moon Mountain made it smaller. Maybe that was why so many people chose to do mediocre things, as long as their friends were doing them too:

it was all about making the circles overlap, even at the expense of greater adventures, even at the expense of life itself.

Ava appeared in the common room doorway wearing one of Nan's old bathrobes, her damp hair giving off a scent of cedar. "Ready for bed?" she said.

"I'll be up in a minute," I said.

But while I was looking at the last of Noe's photos, my mind kept darting to the procedure I was going to have the next morning. What if it hurt? What if something went wrong? I started loading the websites I'd looked at on the day I took the pregnancy test, the ones that explained what was going to happen during the abortion. From there, I started reading stories that other girls had posted, scanning forum threads, clicking link after link, getting more and more wound up until suddenly it was six a.m. and I hadn't even gone to bed.

I shut the laptop. My ears were ringing and my eyes were dry. Climbing the stairs, I could feel the quiet of the house, unbroken by so much as a birdcall. *Four more hours*, I thought, and my heart began to beat so hard I had to pause and lean against the wall.

In Ava's room, I set the laptop on the desk and crept over to her bed. After a moment's hesitation, I shook her shoulder gently.

"Ava?" I said. "I'm scared."

She let out a sleepy murmur and lifted her blanket. I slipped in beside her and she pulled me close. Within a few minutes, pale dawn light was creeping into the room. I had just started to drift off when the first birds of morning began to sing.

59

AVA AND I DIDN'T TALK MUCH on the way to the clinic. I was too nervous, and Ava was still waking up. She sipped the coffee she'd dumped into a travel mug on our way out of the dorm and honked at a trucker who cut us off.

"Dickhead," she grumbled, then, "Sorry, Annabeth. I tend to be a bitch until about noon."

She smiled at me, then patted my leg. "You didn't sleep at all last night, did you?"

I shook my head.

"You think you're scared now," said Ava, "imagine if you didn't have a choice."

She flicked the turn signal on and pulled into the parking lot. "Well, chickie. Here we are."

* * *

The nurse called me in to sign some papers and talk over what was going to happen during the abortion, and then I had to go back out and wait for almost another hour. The waiting room was filled with teenage couples and twentysomething college students and grown women with kids. I wished I'd brought my headphones to tune out all the chaos. Instead, Ava and I hunched over a crossword puzzle in a magazine.

"What if the doctor goes out to lunch before she gets to me?" I kept saying. "Do you think the nurse forgot I'm here?"

"It's okay, Annabeth," Ava said. "The waiting is the worst part. Just remember, by the time you go to sleep tonight, this will be over."

Finally, the nurse came out and called my name. Ava squeezed my hand. "I'll be right here," she said.

In the exam room, I undressed and put on the paper gown the nurse had left for me, then took out the tiny bottle of lavender oil Ava had given me in the car.

"Take a deep breath of this if you're feeling scared," she'd said. "It helps."

Now I dabbed it on my wrists and under my nose, anointing myself like a priestess about to enter a holy mountain. I couldn't believe that in five or ten minutes, this would be over. They would take it out of me, and when I walked out of this room it would not be there anymore. *Good-bye*, I thought, and then there was a knock on the door, and the nurse and doctor came in.

60

AVA'S FRIEND WAS RIGHT. THE awkward, tense, scary thing I'd been bracing myself for all night had barely gotten started when the doctor said, "And we're done."

I couldn't believe how quickly it was over. I kept thinking there were other steps, but no, said the nurse, I was really done.

As I walked out with Ava, the world was bright and snowy, noisy with traffic. I wondered what Noe was doing. I wondered if Mom was having a good day at work. It was amazing that things could go back to normal so quickly. I guess I hadn't realized it, but part of me had expected something terrible to happen. It was taking my brain a moment to get reoriented to the new, disaster-free reality.

I was hungry, and a little crampy, and woozy from the sedative drugs. On the drive home, Ava stopped at a coffee shop to get us blueberry scones. When we got back to the dorm, Ava's roommates had pooled together to buy me flowers. They were sitting in a vase on Ava's desk, dahlias like fireworks, yellow bursting out of pink. *Get Well Soon*, said the card, with a picture of a cartoon frog. *Love, your friends at Mackenzie House.*

"What do you feel like doing now?" said Ava. "Want me to stay with you, or would you rather be alone?"

"I think I want to be alone for a while."

"You can use my computer if you want. Or take a nap or a shower. Eat whatever you want in the kitchen. You know where the tea is, right?"

"Yeah."

She smiled at me, her blue hair bright against the white wall.

Funny, the people you end up being close to in the end.

61

WHEN AVA LEFT, I WENT THE kitchen to make tea. The dorm was quiet. While the water boiled, I took my time choosing from a dozen jars of flaky stuff with names like Peppermint Passion and Ginger Fairy. When my tea was ready, I carried the mug up to Ava's room and started to read one of her theater books.

Outside Ava's window, people were trickling across the quad like colored dots, hurrying to their classes. A few intrepid squirrels were venturing out to inspect post-lunchtime contributions to the garbage cans. I imagined that this was my life. Curling up in a dorm room, reading a smart book, waiting for my friends to get back from their classes so we could cook something delicious and figure out what we were doing that night. On the weekends, I'd go rock climbing or hiking, or lie in the grassy quad watching leaves fall. I wondered if I'd think about this day—if I'd remember myself at seventeen, throwing up on the Greyhound, sliding down Half Moon Mountain, going to the clinic with Ava, sitting on her bed and looking out the window after it was all done.

You're doing okay, I thought to myself, and it was like there was a future Annabeth saying those words inside my head.

It was nice to think there was a future Annabeth who liked me and thought I was okay. It was almost like making a friend.

You're okay, too, I said back, and I put my head on Ava's pillow and fell asleep.

62

WHEN I WOKE UP FROM MY nap, it was almost time to walk to Pauline's house for dinner. I lay on Ava's bed for a while longer, not wanting to get out from under her fuzzy blanket. I was still a little crampy and very tired, and all I wanted was to sleep some more. For a second, I thought about calling Pauline and telling her I couldn't come. But then Pauline would tell Mom I was sick, and Mom would be both curious as to the nature of the illness and disappointed I hadn't seen Pauline.

I got out of bed and took a few of the pills the nurse had given me. *Just go to Pauline's and get it over with*, I thought. At least tomorrow, I wouldn't have to do anything except ride a bus and sleep.

Ava must have come into the room and left again. There was a piece of leftover birthday cake on her desk, with a note that said, *Call me if you need anything!*

I wrapped up the cake and put it in my backpack for the bus ride tomorrow. Who knew? Maybe I would meet someone who needed a magic spirit friend, and I would give it to them.

Pauline lived only a mile from campus, but somehow the walk drained the life out of me. It felt like the day had already lasted a hundred years. I wanted to talk to myself some more; to attend to those quiet inner stirrings that didn't happen every day. I wasn't ready to turn outward, to engage.

It's just dinner, I told myself. *Do it for Mom.*

I rustled up a smile and rang the doorbell.

"ANNABETH!" EXCLAIMED PAULINE, SWINGING
open her front door that was festooned with a wreath and a
clutch of jingling bells. "Come on in."

Pauline was shorter than me by a few inches. She was fond
of long skirts and linen shirts with wooden beads for buttons. Mom had told me that Pauline had been in Earth First!
in college and chained herself to a tree. Now she was a lawyer
for an environmental nonprofit and fought for the trees in a
courtroom instead. When I was little, I thought Pauline was
weird because she brought her own food when she came to
visit us, sacks of bulgur wheat and lentils and seaweed, as if she
was going on a camping trip and not visiting someone's house.

What was wrong with frozen pizza from No Frills?

Pauline and Mom went to high school together, but Pauline hadn't lived in our town since before I was born. When she came to visit, it always used to surprise me that she knew where everything was; that it was her town, too, from a previous lifetime. It bothered me that people could have repertoires of towns; I found it slightly offensive. In my childish way, I told myself Mom and I were superior. Sometimes after Pauline's visits, Mom would talk about finishing her paramedic training and "traveling around a little" after I went away to college. This always freaked me out. Not the going-away-to-college part, which was still a distant abstraction, but that Mom might pack up our little house and go away too. *I need you* here, I would say, and stamp my foot. As if Mom going anywhere would unhinge east from west, and I wouldn't be able to find myself anymore.

Pauline's house was small and warm and wood-paneled. I recognized a few of Mom's paintings on the walls. There was a Christmas tree in the corner and a big, drooling dog dozing on the couch. Pauline's husband, Lev, was in the kitchen chopping parsley.

"Leslie told me you're vegetarian," Pauline said. "I hope falafel's okay. Can I get you something to drink? Water, tea, juice?"

"Just water, please."

She disappeared into the kitchen, and I sat on the couch

with the dog. There was a box of records on the floor. I fingered their narrow spines. Bob Dylan, Peter, Paul and Mary, Ani DiFranco. Pauline's couch was big and comfortable, with a thick blanket folded up on one end. I wondered whether Mom would have a house like this if she hadn't had me. If Mom would have a life like this.

"So, tell me about your visit to Northern," said Pauline, coming back with two glasses of water and a little bowl of snack mix on a tray. "Did Ava take you to Half Moon Mountain?"

I sipped my water and did my best to chat with her. Pauline still had a long braid that went down to her waist, a braid I loved to play with when I was little. When she used to visit us, we would play Climbing Trees and Building Forts and, if it was winter, Dragging the Injured Hiker on a Sled. Things were more fun when Pauline was around. When it was Pauline's turn to be the Injured Hiker, Mom would get a wild look in her eye and we would pull the sled as fast as we could, giggling like crazy until somebody fell down or the sled tipped over.

"Do you know what you want to study?" Pauline was saying.

"Maybe forestry," I said.

It felt like only 1 percent of me was actually talking to Pauline, and the other 99 percent was doing anything it could to acquire sleep. The pattern on the blanket was swimming before my eyes. "Take it easy for a day or two," the nurse had said. "No sledding." I wanted to be back in Ava's room, curled up in her bed. *It was stupid to come here, stupid stupid stupid.*

Pauline was waiting for me to say something.

"Can I use your bathroom?" I said.

"Sure."

Pauline showed me the way. I locked myself in and washed my face, trying to wake myself up with the cold water. I remembered the time in tenth grade when I'd found Noe and this girl Dulcie Simmonds from choir in the downstairs girls' bathroom, the tiled room echoing with Dulcie's sobs. I joined them at the sink.

"What's wrong?" I'd said.

Noe had her arm around Dulcie's back.

"Dulcie's pregnant," Noe informed me.

"What?!"

Dulcie's face in the mirror was splotchy and pink. The paper towel dispenser was all the way dispensed. After school that day, I went with them to the drugstore and then to Dulcie's house and sat on her enormous frilly bed while Noe herded her into the bathroom, listening to their voices through the half-open bathroom door. Laughter, too. As if this were a game, another girlish adventure. And maybe it was.

"Pee on it," Noe was saying. "Aim, girl." They'd exploded into giggles.

"I can't aim when you're—"

Giggles, giggles. I'd looked around Dulcie's room. She had very few books, just a closet and a wardrobe and a desk covered with framed family photographs and ballerina figurines, all sorts of shoes lined up against her bedroom wall: red satin high heels, knee-high boots in black leather, blue plastic sandals, black pumps with feathery stuff on the toes. They looked like the props in a magician's bag, the hoops and wands and handkerchiefs necessary to a life based on illusion. Mom and I had one pair of shoes each, three if you counted hiking boots and sandals for summer.

Jubilant shrieks. "Oh, thank God!"

And Noe, drily, "Congratulations. Your oven has been certified bunless."

I smiled, imagining Noe saying that to me: *Congratulations. Your oven has been certified bunless.* And smiled again, remembering how Noe had informed me, later, that Dulcie Simmonds had never even had all-the-way sex, could not possibly have been pregnant, and was making the whole thing up for drama: *Unless there is something really weird going on with Mark DiNadio's tongue, in which case all bets are off.*

I sat on the edge of the tub for a few minutes to rest. The smell of the dinner Lev was cooking crept in under the door. I could hear them talking in the kitchen. *Just act normal*, I thought. *You can sleep soon.*

When I came out of the bathroom, Pauline poked her head out of the kitchen. "Dinner's on the table," she said brightly.

I followed them into the dining room and we all sat down to eat. We chatted about the Wilda McClure house and the theater lecture Ava had taken me to, and I managed to eat most of my falafel and tabbouleh, but by the time Lev went into the kitchen for the blueberry pie, I was spent.

"Pauline?" I said. "I need to lie down."

Scraping of chairs, worried murmurs, the blueberry pie hustled back into the kitchen. I thought I would die of embarrassment.

"I thought you looked a little sick," said Pauline.

We went out to the living room and I lay down on the couch beside the drooling dog. Pauline draped the patterned blanket over my shoulders. I wanted to sleep for ten thousand years. I hadn't realized how worried I'd been until the appointment was over. Now that the burden had been removed, I felt its full weight for the first time.

I must have looked awful.

"Do you want to call your mom?" Pauline said.

"No."

"Are you sure?"

She reached for the phone. I grabbed her hand to stop her.

"Please don't call her," I said.

Sharp silence. Something changed in the air. I took my hand off Pauline's, but it was too late. She sank to a crouch beside me and patted the dog's head.

"Annabeth," said Pauline. "I think you'd better tell me what's going on."

I KEPT THE STORY SIMPLE. HOMECOMING dance,
boy, accident. I tried to make it sound as adult and reasonable
as possible.

"I didn't want to miss campus visits, so I decided to get it
done while I was up here."

Pauline wasn't buying it.

"Why didn't you tell Leslie?" she said, flat out, when I had
finished my summary.

I skirted my eyes away from Pauline's and started to ram-
ble. Mom and I had been fighting, Mom didn't like my friends,
Mom would freak out if she discovered that I'd spent homecoming drinking Jack Daniel's and Gatorade with a boy I

hardly knew, let alone the sex part.

"I'd already sort of denied that I'd been with a boy," I said. "And then this happened and I didn't want—I couldn't stand—for her to look at me like that."

"Look at you like what?" Pauline said.

"Like a disappointment," I said. "Like a skank."

"Is that how you see yourself?"

"No."

"Then why would Leslie?"

I mumbled something about Operation Condom Drop. The truth is, *skank* wasn't the thing I was worried about. It was something else. It was the cold glove that clenched at my stomach when I tried to finish my sandwiches. The way I sometimes saw myself in the mirror and wondered if Mom saw him when she looked at me. The way that revulsion would sometimes overcome me when I was in the shower or getting dressed for school, the tightness that lived in the corner of my heart, as if something there could hardly stand to be alive.

"I don't want to give her any more reasons to hate me," I said.

Pauline's gray-blue eyes gazed deeply into mine. "Why would she hate you?"

"Why do you think?"

The clock on the mantelpiece ticked. The dog snored. Pauline drew in a short breath. "Leslie once told me she would rather crawl barefoot through snow than see you suffering. She loves you more than anyone else in the world. It's a spit in her face to say she wouldn't want to be with you for every minute that you were going through this. A spit in the face."

I wasn't expecting Pauline to be angry. I lay there, stunned, while she got up and disappeared into the kitchen.

I pulled the blanket up to my chin. I wasn't sure which was worse: the grief I imagined in my mother's voice when she said this, or the love. I didn't want to be responsible for either. I just wanted to disappear.

"I'd like you to sleep here tonight," Pauline said when she came back. "Can you call your cousin to let her know?"

Knowing better than to argue with her, I pulled out my phone.

65

BEFORE SAYING GOOD NIGHT, PAULINE gave me
an ultimatum.

"I want you to tell her," she said. "It's not the kind of decision you're supposed to make for another person, and you can
call me a blackmailing bitch, but there is no way I'm putting
you on a bus tomorrow in your condition. We'll call her in the
morning and you can explain."

Pauline looked tired. She stood in the doorway of the den
with her arms folded.

"You can hate me if you need to," Pauline said. "If I was
your age I'd hate me too. Leslie would never forgive me if I let
you keep this a secret from her. I guess that's more important to

me than being the cool auntie, even though I wish there was a way I could be both."

She smiled sadly. I dropped onto the foldout couch and felt my world sink like a flooded canoe. Pauline came over and gave me a half hug.

"She loves you," Pauline said. "I love you too."

The pattern in the floor danced and flashed. I thought forlornly of the flowers on Ava's desk. I nodded, and Pauline went away.

EVEN THOUGH I WAS ALMOST DELIRIOUS from
exhaustion, there was no way I could sleep with the phone
call hanging over my head. I woke up Pauline's computer and
browsed distractedly. I started looking at old photos of Noe
and me, the ones I used to upload religiously: Noe and Annabeth drinking lemonade on Noe's patio, Noe and Annabeth
making scared faces on a roller coaster, Noe and Annabeth
wearing matching *Trivia Wars* T-shirts in tenth grade. I was
so deep in my memories that when Noe chatted me I almost
jumped out of my chair.

hey doll. how's it going?

good, I typed. **well—**

yeah. good.

what's up?

I hesitated, my hands hovering over the keyboard.

remember how you said the pill still worked if you took half?
I typed.

well

it doesn't.

It took a few seconds for Noe to reply, and when she did it was first just a stream of exclamation points.

!!!

!!!!!!!

!!!!!!!!!!!

ohmigod!!!!!

i know, I typed.

what are you going to do?!?!??

i already did it

this morning

are you ok?!?!?

yeah

are you sure???

oh bethy. i want to give you the biggest hug right now

this year has been so crazy

i know, I typed.

i want to wrap you up in a warm blanket

and rub your ears

and tell you everything is going to be okay

it is ok

i had my cousin

and all her friends were really nice

i'm so relieved it's over

you should have told me

we could have talked about it

how far along were you?

nine weeks

ohmigod

so you were pregnant on halloween

and thanksgiving

and nobody knew it

crazy, right?

i need to go

can we talk in the morning?

might be hard

but i'll try

are you sure you're ok?

i just can't—

god. wow.

i am sitting here in shock.

see you soon

yes! soon. i can't believe we have school on monday.

i can't believe it either

oh bethy. oh dear.

talk to you tomorrow, k?

ok

After talking to Noe, I still couldn't sleep. I got up from the computer and started rummaging through Pauline's books. The den seemed like more of a storage room; Pauline had moved cardboard boxes of books aside to fold out the bed. I pulled down one book and then another one, making a little stack to take to the couch with me. The cardboard boxes were mostly photography books; I dug through them and pulled out one about the boreal forest and one about polar bears. I was at the bottom of the photography box when my eye fell on a spine that wasn't like the others. It was a scruffy journal held together by sagging elastic. I slid it out from between its neighbors and flipped it over.

Nature Notes, said the cardboard cover. I slid off the elastic and opened it.

Property of Pauline Delacruz, said the inside page, with a date from a summer eighteen years ago. When I turned the page, a dried maple leaf fell out.

Algonquin Paddle-o-Rama, said the first entry. *Day Uno. Saw three moose, a bear, and a beaver. Tipped canoe, cookies lost, hot dogs salvaged. Rachel and Claire sang a war song, Pete and Gary banged the drums. Leslie cooked bannock with chocolate chips, yum.*

I smiled at the mention of Mom, a smile that froze at the next sentence:

Our Fearless Leader Scott "J-Stroke" McLaughlin can't read map, driving everyone crazy with inane route suggestions. Must cast him onto next mosquito-infested island, lighten load.

I sank onto the foldout bed, my ears ringing.

Scott McLaughlin. Mom. Canoe trip.

I wasn't sure I could read this.

Day 2 yielded blue herons and lily pads, Day 3 *Lev stung by a bee, Doctor Pauline administered dose of whiskey*, Day 4 *Green Canoe Crew fell victim to Galloping Trots*, Day 5, snapping turtles and seven-foot moose, *Whiskey flowed at campfire, all were raucous and wild. much hooting and dancing. stumbled to bed.*

Day 6, *Leslie acting weird, says she got her period. offered secret chocolate stash to no avail.* Day 7, *rain, thunderstorms, everyone miserable.* Day 8, *heading in.*

There were some loose photographs tucked into the back of the journal. Pauline and Lev, paddling canoes. Mom building a fire. And one of the whole group: Mom, Pauline, Lev, a few women I didn't recognize, a few men who couldn't possibly be him (too young, too old, wrong skin color), and one boy in red swim trunks with hairy legs, who was the right age and the right color and had a face shaped just like mine. I found his name in the list written under the photograph.

Asshole, I thought to myself as angry tears pricked at my eyes. *Asshole. Asshole. Asshole.*

Could a word reach through space and time to burn someone? I hoped it could. I hoped he could feel the heat of it on
the back of his neck. I hoped wherever he was, he knew how
thoroughly he was hated.

I slipped the journal into my backpack and lay on the bed.

All I knew was I wanted to go home.

61

IN THE MORNING, THE CRAMPS HAD dimmed. My phone was crammed with texts from Noe:

are you ok???

so worried.

where are you???

Noe seemed to think I'd come close to dying. I wasn't sure why. Maybe there was a famous movie where the girl died, or she was imagining a more dramatic procedure than had actually taken place.

i'm fine, I texted back.

i have to call my mom now.

poor dear.

thinking about you.

call me as soon as you get home.

When I ventured into the kitchen, Pauline was boiling a pot of herbs on the stove for me to drink. I thought of Ava's roommate. I guess some of that stuff was good to do and some of it wasn't. Pauline said it was mostly chamomile, with valerian to help me relax.

"Sometimes I forget what it feels like to be seventeen. I fought with my mom all the time," said Pauline.

"What about?" I said.

Pauline rolled her eyes. "Clothes. Music. Swearing. Lev."

We sat in her kitchen eating muffins that Lev had baked that morning. I started to think that Pauline had changed her mind about calling Mom and the knot in my stomach relaxed, but after we'd finished our muffins Pauline reached for the phone.

"Are you ready?" she said, then shook her head. "Stupid question."

Mom drives a lot faster than a bus, especially when she's angry.

She cried, called me an idiot, and said she would be there in five hours.

WHEN I HEARD THE CAR DOOR slam in Pauline's driveway, my heart jumped. A few seconds later, Mom burst into the house without knocking. Her hair was disheveled and she hadn't taken the time to grab a sweater even though it was ten below. Our eyes met, and it was like someone had switched on a heat lamp. My body went hot all the way from my hair follicles to my intestines.

"I can't believe you," she shouted, and then she wrapped me in a hug that almost knocked me down.

69

I WANTED TO ASK HER ABOUT the boy in red swim trunks.

I wanted to tell her about the cold hand and the sandwich halves.

I wanted to explain that ever since Ava had told me (I only ever thought about Ava telling me, even though the two tellings happened within a week), my body couldn't always summon the energy to eat or bleed. That it wanted to shrink, even though I coaxed it to grow.

I wanted to explain that if I hid things from her, it was because I couldn't stand to see Mom hurting any more than she could stand it in me.

It was winter-mixing. Rain mixed with snow. The trees were a runny green slurry coursing past the car windows. After the initial explosion, things had calmed down, and we'd all gone out to lunch. Mom and Pauline had griped about the stupidity of teenage boys and talked about the things they'd tried to hide from their parents in high school. Afterward I took a nap, and Mom and Pauline had talked in the kitchen for another two hours. Pauline wanted us to stay over, but Mom had to work in the morning. We drove to Ava's dorm to pick up my things, and I'd scrawled a note for Ava on the back of an envelope.

Thanks for everything. Half Moon Mountain was the best. Then we'd left.

Now Mom was being too quiet.

"Where does he live?" I said.

"Who?"

"Scott."

Long pause. I looked down at my lap, conscious of having invoked a demon. At the sound of his name I could feel the car fill with icy air. *Sorry sorry sorry*, I thought, wishing I could take it back.

It was always like this, on the extremely rare occasion I tried to talk about him with Mom. Like lifting a rock to see the insects underneath, and seeing them scurry around in a panic. Feeling bad because all they wanted to do was stay safely hidden under their rock. Sometimes I felt like Mom regretted telling me. At least my questions back then were dumb and harmless, not these ambushes that made her think about a person she'd rather forget.

Sorry sorry sorry, I thought, *sorry sorry sorry*.

I don't know why I thought it was a good time to try for a conversation. Maybe because things were already so raw.

Mom named a suburb of a suburb of a big city an hour and a half from our town. "Why do you want to know?" she said tightly.

"No reason," I peeped.

I squished myself against the window and stared at the road.

70

FALLING ROCKS, SAID THE SIGNS, AND I wanted to be one, tumbling angry forever.

YOU ARE IN BEAR COUNTRY, said the signs, and I wanted to lumber down riverbeds in pajamas of meat and fur.

ICE ON ROADS, said the signs, and I wanted to be that deadly, to kill without warning, out of nowhere, invisibly.

The city said ENTER, the bridge said MAX WEIGHT 1.5 TONS, and I felt myself heavy, breaking the spans.

I flinched when we passed a sign that said the name of his town.

I could feel him in the car with us, sucking up all the air.

I wanted to push him out the door, but I didn't know how.

71

WHEN IT GOT DARK, WE STOPPED at a diner in a town I didn't recognize. We ordered tomato soup. Neither of us was very hungry. It came with hard white bread rolls and frozen packets of butter on a plate.

"Are you mad at me?" I said.

"I don't know yet."

We ate our soup in silence. The waiter came by with more coffee for Mom. I listened to it splashing into her mug. Behind us, a pair of truckers was watching a football game on TV. I thought about the regional park. It seemed like there was always a sports game going on in the background when Mom and I were having a bad time. I snuck a peek at her face. The emotions there were too complicated for me to read. Strain.

Exhaustion. Exasperation. Hurt. I looked back at my soup and felt the minutes drag.

"I guess it's my fault for embarrassing you with the condoms," Mom blurted at last. "How were you supposed to tell me after that?"

I blushed. I couldn't stand to see her feeling guilty for something I'd done.

"How long did you know?" said Mom.

It was a relief to be talking again. Better than that long, strained silence in which God-knows-what thoughts could be lurking. "Only since the day before I left for Maple Bay."

Mom shook her head. "Jesus," she said. "Well, at least you were somewhat responsible. Ava's not the worst person you could have asked to help you. And Pauline says you didn't even try to lie to her. I'm just sorry you didn't feel like you could tell me."

"I'm sorry too."

Our eyes met over the empty soup bowls and then we both looked away, as if the pain of connection was too piercing to sustain. My mother and I loved each other with eyes averted, like birds circling a pile of grain but never coming close enough to peck. As if love was a mirage that could shimmer and vanish if you looked at it too closely, or a tree with sorrow nesting in every branch: shake it too hard and your heart would break.

We walked to the cold car and got back on the road.

It was too dark to see the trees now, and soon we were home.

72

I TOLD NOE IT WAS TOO late to come over, but she insisted.

"Mom?" I said sheepishly, hovering in her bedroom door. "Noe's coming by for a few minutes. I think we're going to go for a walk."

Mom grumbled her acquiescence, and I went downstairs to wait by the window until I saw Noe appear at the end of the block. I slipped out the door and ran to meet her. Our bodies collided, and I thought of the loons who wheeled through our town on their annual migration until one year, for no reason anyone could discern, they didn't come back.

"Bethy," she gasped.

"Noe," I wailed.

The street at night was empty and quiet, the moon a sliver.

I wondered what it would be like not to know her anymore.

73

THE WEEK AFTER CAMPUS VISITS, OUR school was buzzing with stories of what everyone had gotten up to. Michael Lavelle had gotten drunk with a college basketball team and woke up with a string bikini drawn over his nipples in permanent marker. Eleanor Watchless had attended a 400-level physics seminar and astounded the professor by turning in the solution to every problem she had written on the board. Mallory Davis had cheated on Tim Xiu with her campus tour guide.

Steven had taken the train south to NYU to check out their drama department. In Art, he chattered about it nonstop. "It's like an entire school full of pee sisters," he confessed gleefully. "Perhaps an entire city." He'd stayed with his rich uncle in Manhattan, and the uncle had taken him to see *The Lion King*, *Avenue Q*, and a ballet called *Petrushka*. He brandished a pink slipper the lead dancer had signed for him after the show. After Art, we went to the bathroom together to wash the paint off our hands, an endeavor that proved to be surprisingly labor-intensive.

"What about you, Annabeth?" Steven said. "You're being awfully quiet about Northern."

"It was—very interesting," I said.

"Interesting how?"

"A lot of ways. Every way."

I pumped more soap into my hands and scrubbed at my fingernails, which were caked with tenacious blue paint. I thought we'd reverted to friendly silence, but after a moment Steven said, "Are you going to tell me about it, or is the privilege reserved for first-degree friends?"

"Steven—" I groaned.

"I'm right, aren't I? Whatever it is, you probably told Noe the minute you saw her, but I'm just the person you kill time with in Art."

I froze, hot water blasting over my hands. "We *are* friends," I said. "We talk all the time."

"*I* talk all the time," said Steven. "You demur."

"I'm sorry," I said. "I guess I'm a private person."

"A picket fence is private. You're the freaking Berlin Wall."

I blushed hard. I remembered the way Noe's gym friends

had badgered me at the restaurant, the night of the homecoming dance: *Why are you so quiet? Why don't you ever talk?* I hadn't managed to make a connection with them, and apparently I'd been kidding myself about making a connection with Steven.

"Don't you think I'd talk if I could?" I said.

"Why can't you?"

The bathroom tiles were flecked with shiny bits of copper. I'd never noticed that before. My hands were red and throbbing from being under the hot water for too long. I was thinking about Scott's face in the camping trip photograph. Maybe I'd never be normal. Maybe I'd never have a real friend. Steven was right. Friendship was more than laughing at someone's jokes. It was more like skinny-dipping: if you cheated and kept a piece of clothing on, you'd never experience the wonder of the water against your bare skin, or be a full participant in the trust that binds naked swimmers to one another.

"I'm not like you and Noe," I said. "Sometimes I feel like everyone else has this *thing* that I'm missing."

On *thing*, my hand moved to the place on my rib cage where my heart used to live. I drew it away quickly.

"Do you really believe that?" said Steven.

"If someone amputated your leg, would you *believe* that you still had it?" I said.

The bathroom door creaked open, and Kaylee and

Rhiannon walked in with a few other girls. I busied myself with the paper towel dispenser.

"Hey, Kaylee, hey, Rhiannon," I said.

"Hey, Anna—gross, what's *he* doing in here?"

I glanced at Steven. "Pee Sisters Convention," I sighed. "We were just leaving."

On the way down the hall, Steven gave me a high five. "That was great," he said.

"What was great?"

"We had a fight. You said things."

He seemed to consider this a victory, but my shoulders slumped.

"I still haven't told you about Northern," I burst out. "And I've never made it . . . *okay* . . . for you to be anything other than a funny person in Art. You could be going through hell right now and I wouldn't even know, because I've made it so clear that *funny person in Art* is the only part you're allowed to play."

We paused outside the cafeteria. The bulletin boards were cluttered with announcements for the winter talent show and the holiday concert and sign-ups for the annual ski trip.

"I *suck*," I said. "It's like I'm not even human. You've been trying so hard to be friends with me, and I haven't been a friend to you."

Steven could tell he'd triggered something bigger than he'd

intended. He reached out and gently touched my sleeve. "The thing that's actually wrong with you is probably tiny to non-existent compared to the things you've made yourself believe are wrong with you. At least, that's what Ricardo says."

"What if the thing is big?" I said. "And it's not in your imagination?"

The bell began to ring for fourth period. We turned from the cafeteria without going in and walked back down the hall. For once, the space between us was heavy and quiet instead of being filled with witty banter.

It felt strange, the heaviness and quiet. It scared me.

Some kinds of scary are better than others, I guess. When I sank into my desk for Media Studies, I felt like a swimmer come in from the sea.

DECEMBER WAS COLD AND WHITE AND blinding.
The trees bent and creaked under the weight of the snow. I
tried to get excited about exams and Secret Santas and all that
stuff, but it was hard.

In Art, Mr. Lim called me up to his desk. "Ms. Schultz, you
have a redo outstanding on your self-portrait." At lunch, I filled
a jar with rocks and left it in his office with a title card that said,
*RAW MATERIALS II: Portrait of the Artist as a Jar Full of
Stones.* It would make a nice diptych, I thought.

I got an email from Loren Wilder, my tour guide from
Northern. *Thought you might be interested in this poem by
Wilda McClure.* He signed the message with a smiley and his

initials. I wondered how he had gotten my email address, then remembered it was on the form Mom had filled out to book the tour.

The poem was about wolves in a castle of wind. I tried to read it, but zoned out after a line or two.

I guess I wasn't in the mood for poetry just then.

Noe was always busy studying with friends from her classes. In Art, Steven showed me the Christmas present he was making for her: a leotard with purple and silver feathers, which he was calling the Noe Suit. I told him about Ava and Pauline, and let him smell the bottle of lavender oil Ava had given me before the abortion. He wanted some on his wrists. I dabbed it on carefully.

"Who smells like perfume?" Noe said later as we walked down the hall.

I was feeling bad about putting off Bob for so long, so I stopped by his office with a list of vegetarian food requests for the cafeteria. He was in the sagging swivel chair studying for a nutritionist exam and listening to a program on NPR.

"What happened to *Kingdom of Stones*?" I said.

"I finished it. Do you want to borrow the CDs?"

I was going to say no, but changed my mind. "Sure."

He rummaged around in the desk and handed me a five-disc box. "Don't start listening before you've finished exams. The story is very addictive."

"Okay," I said.

* * *

On the last day of exams, Noe, Steven, and I went downtown to use up my pizza coupons. It turned out the pizzeria in question was a dingy joint beside the Anaconda Nite Club. The hairy-browed guy at the cash register looked at my coupons, flicked them back across the counter, and said, "Nice-a try, kids. These-a been expired for three years."

"Trust a fake nutritionist," Noe said as we trudged out.

"I thought it was weird that he had so many," I said.

I told myself I was doing okay. I went skating at the rink and Christmas shopping at the mall and even to a party at Lindsay Harris's house. I pulled the craft supply box out of the closet and made Noe a jeweled box for the talcum powder she put on her hands for uneven bars, and Steven a sparkly headband that said PEE SISTERS in purple sequins.

One day when I was cleaning my room, I found the postcards I'd bought at the Wilda McClure house. I took them downstairs and gave them to Mom.

"These are for you," I said.

"Oh," she said. She stuck them to the fridge with magnets. A forest, a lake, a beaver dam, a pair of snowshoes. They looked small and dumb on the fridge, doing nothing to conjure the wilderness I'd glimpsed from the bus window.

We had been careful with each other since Maple Bay. Overly polite. She took me to see a doctor to "check things out," and on the way home we hardly spoke. I wanted to tell her about the journal I had found, but I knew it would only make her sad. Instead, I carried around the image of Scott's face like a stone lodged in my throat.

I looked up his address on the internet. It wasn't very hard, since I had his full name and the town.

It was strange to think of him having a house and a car and a whole normal life. It made me angry. It creeped me out.

I fantasized that I was on the canoe trip with Mom and Pauline and I came to Mom's rescue. In some versions, I whacked him over the head with a paddle. In other versions I came running with a can of bear spray.

Sometimes in my dreams, I killed him over and over again, but he kept on getting up like a zombie and there was no way to make him die.

75

THAT CHRISTMAS, THE WATERFALL FROZE for the first time in two hundred years. The whole town came out to peer at it: a palace of ice, intricate and spired and still, so terribly still, where we had only ever seen it tumble and churn. I went with Mom and Nan and Aunt Monique to huddle by the iron railing and take turns saying how we'd never, ever, ever, seen a thing like that before.

At Nan's house, presents. We ate the gingerbread my cousin Max had baked, and Uncle Dylan plunked out "We Three Kings" on the old piano. Ava had stayed in Maple Bay to volunteer at a women's shelter over Christmas. She called, and Uncle

Dylan passed the phone around, but it was hard to talk with everybody there. Then Aunt Monique's parents came over, Max and Ava's other grandparents, the ones who were horrified that Mom didn't give me up for adoption, and still acted stiff and uncomfortable around me, although they tried to be nice. They said hello and asked me about school, but I could tell I made them nervous, and we all excused ourselves from the conversation as fast as we could.

I wondered what Scott was doing, and what my other grandparents were doing, the ones I'd never met. I sat on the edge of Nan's plaid couch and fussed with the fireplace, adding logs and blowing on the coals and moving things around.

"Annabeth," called Mom. "It's your turn for charades."

The card I pulled was *Star Wars*. Star: a finger pointing at the sky. Wars: an imaginary gun firing willy-nilly.

"Sky shooter!" everyone shouted. "Battle sky!"

I was glad when the whole thing was over.

A COUPLE OF DAYS LATER I packed my backpack, told
Mom I was going to Noe's, and walked two miles to the station to catch a bus to a suburb of a suburb of a suburb of a big
city an hour and a half east. I didn't trust myself to drive, and
what if the Honda broke down along the way? My hands trembled in my lap. The highway flashed past outside the window,
miles and miles of dreary asphalt, the warehouses and factory
stores annihilating the landscape. I spread my notebook open
on my knees and wrote letter after ink-smeared letter. *You're a
bastard*, I wrote, *a horrible bastard. I hope you die.* I signed the
final one *Leslie's daughter*, folded it up, and put it in the outside
pocket of my coat.

When I got off the bus, it was twilight. I walked another two miles, following the directions I'd written on a piece of paper. The house was at the end of a wide, curving street with lots of landscaping. As I approached, my breath got ragged and short. I gripped the rock in my pocket—somehow, the sword of my fantasies had failed to materialize—and felt its coldness and hardness rise through my skin to surround me like a shield.

Hey, I would shout. *Do you know who I am?*

Smash! Blood and brains! Moaning pleas for forgiveness!

A car pulled into the driveway of the house as I was walking past it. A man got out. Tall, thin. Handsome. As he walked to his front door, he gave me a neighborly wave.

"Beautiful night," he said.

Finish him. "Yeah," I said, and kept walking.

He went into his house. I walked faster. The trees on his street were covered in frost. It made them shimmer in the moonlight like something out of a dream.

When I came to the end of the block I stopped on the sidewalk. Cold air knifed into my lungs with every breath. There were frozen candy bar wrappers in the gutter that reminded me of the first day of school. Frozen ghosts with nowhere left to go. A truck drove past that reminded me of Mom's: rusty tailpipe, rattly bed. I hesitated a moment longer, the rock damp and jagged against my palm, then turned around and walked quickly and deliberately back to Scott's house. His curtains were closed.

The car in his driveway was new, glossy. A nice suburban car. A nice suburban house. There were strings of Christmas lights wrapped around his front bushes, the bulbs glowing greenly through the snow.

I could have stared at the house all night: wondering, watching, gathering anger like fistfuls of cotton fluff. But then a light turned on upstairs. It startled me. Reminded me where I was.

I threw the rock at his front window and heard it shatter.

I wished I could have saved a piece of the glass, but I was running hard hard hard until the lights of the main road, and I didn't even think about getting a souvenir until it was too late.

77

I CAUGHT THE NEXT BUS BACK to my town and hugged my backpack against me the whole way. My ears were ringing. Adrenaline made my arms and legs both rigid and loose, like I was either going to harden into a statue or melt into a puddle.

I didn't know why I had gone there. I didn't know why I had thrown the rock.

The December moon was cold and brittle.

The heater vents blew stale breath at my head.

The bus was half an hour from my town when I reached into my pocket and realized the letter had fallen out.

WHEN THE BUS PULLED INTO THE station there was
a scurrying thing in my stomach like a hamster was trapped
inside there. What if he found the letter? What if he called the
police?

That would be rich. Scott calling the police.

My hands were sweaty and slick inside my mittens. I
crouched in the parking lot and dug a handful of gravel out
from under the snow and put it in my mouth. It tasted like
exhaust. In *How to Survive in the Woods*, Wilda McClure says
that sucking on stones can stave off hunger and thirst, but
only for a little while. I should have walked to Scott's house,
I thought to myself. I should have trekked for days with only

stones to suck on, ground them in my teeth until they were sharp as daggers, then walked right up to him and spat them in his face.

I wasn't ready to go home yet, so I walked around the old cemetery that's across the street from the bus station, sucking on my mouthful of gravel and wondering what it would be like to die of starvation. The headstones were sunk deep in the snow. Some of them had frozen flowers piled on top of them. I imagined myself as a zombie-wraith, haunting this town. The old revulsion was seeping up from inside me, like a clogged bathtub drain I shouldn't have disturbed.

I couldn't be like Noe or Steven, I thought to myself. I would never be warm like that, or happy like that, or so certain of my place in the world, so *entitled*. I thought of them under the trees at the park, dappled light on the backs of their sweaters.

My phone rang. I tensed, my mind swinging irrationally to the thought that it was Scott (how would he have my number?) or the police. But when I looked at the tiny screen, it was Ava. I spat out my mouthful of gravel and pressed the yes button with a mittened finger.

"Hey, chickie," Ava said.

It was weird to be talking to Ava in the snowy cemetery, at midnight. I sank against a tree and pressed the cold phone against my ear.

"Hey, Ava."

"How are you?"

How was I? I scuffed my boots at the snow. It was hard to switch from being deep in my head to talking on the phone, to *vocalizing*. Words felt clunky and crude, like using wooden blocks to communicate. How could I explain these things to another human using wooden blocks? Build a tower? Juggle them?

The night had been beautiful. Icicles glittered on the trees. The sky was clear and star-studded over the rooftops, and muted window light glowed on the snow. What did it mean that the world could be beautiful and also contain horrible things?

"I'm fine," I said.

Fine? Was that the best I could do? I wondered if everyone walked around with a muzzle that filtered out all but the most banal of statements, leaving all that was rough, contradictory, or confusing to collect inside them until there was almost no room left to file it. *I broke Scott's window*, I wanted myself to want to say. But something in me butted up to stop any such gesture of intimacy. Even with Ava. Maybe especially with Ava.

"How's school?" Ava said. "Did you finish your college applications?"

I watched a stray cat dart across the road. Another bus rasped into the station, its tires coated in grit. Slowly, I arranged my brain into normal conversation mode.

"I had to write an essay about my campus visit," I said. "A blog post, actually. For the E. O. James blog. Did you know E. O. James had a blog?"

"How twenty-first century," Ava said.

"We had to talk about either the dorms, the campus, the food, or one other thing I can't remember. The bathrooms maybe? Or the library?"

"Proximity to bars that don't card?"

"Maybe that was it."

"I never got to take you to the Sun Dog," Ava said. "If you end up coming here, I call dibs on your initiation. They have a jukebox that plays a hundred percent Neil Young."

"My mom would love that."

"She's probably been there. You should ask. I bet she and Pauline used to go there all the time."

The mention of Mom and Pauline made me think about how Noe wasn't applying to Northern like we'd planned. I let out a whimper in spite of myself.

"What's wrong?" said Ava.

"I just can't believe Noe's not coming with me."

"You'll make tons of friends."

"I know. But you don't understand. I already have all these amazing *memories* of me and Noe going to college together, and now they're not even going to happen."

"Maybe you needed to imagine those things more than you needed to actually do them," said Ava. "The same way that kids make elaborate plans about running away to desert islands."

I didn't like the implication that Noe's and my plans for our college dorm room and Paris and the restaurant with the tiny spoons were anything like a desert island fantasy. Was I the only person in the world who was actually serious about the plans that everyone else blew around for fun?

The poise I had drummed up for the phone call was slipping away fast. My mouth tasted like gravel. My mind was turning back to Scott's house, to everything that was wrong with my life.

"I have to go, Ava," I said. "My phone's almost out of battery."

"Don't be a stranger."

"I won't."

I put my phone back in my pocket and walked out the wrought-iron cemetery gate. My boots sounded harsh against the messy crust of ice that covered the sidewalk. After talking to Ava, I felt like even more of a hypocrite.

A broken window. What was a stupid window? If I was brave, I thought, I would have said something. Why hadn't I said something? When it came down to it, I was no better than the girls at the ice-cream shop where I worked in the summer, simpering and cooing at whatever asshole with four dollars happened to walk into the store. Being nice and polite just because I'd been raised that way, nodding and saying *Yeah* to a freaking rapist because there was no entry in the ice-cream girl playbook for *Fuck you, burn in hell*, the ax in the forehead, the sword in the heart.

There was something out there, something larger than me. A suffocating thing, like ropes that only got tighter the more you wriggled against them.

I should have thrown it at his head, I thought, and something inside me howled and howled and howled until I thought I would hear it howling my whole life.

FOR THE NEXT FEW DAYS, I floated along on a tide of numbness. I went to the New Year's Eve concert with Noe and Steven and everyone else from our school and froze in the snow while a B-list band made love to their microphones. I went to the mall with Nan and froze in the dressing room while she handed post-Christmas sale sweaters over the door. I shoveled the driveway with Mom, the whole world reduced to the sound of scraping metal and thudding boots, and afterward froze in the kitchen waiting for the water to boil for tea.

Finally, it was time to go back to school.

"One more semester," said Mom. "And then graduation!"

She squeezed my shoulders. Walking down the driveway, I slipped on a patch of ice and almost fell.

IT FELT LIKE THE WHOLE WORLD had gone crazy over Christmas break. There was something in the air, I guess, or maybe the frozen waterfall had messed with people's brains. Noe and Steven had run into Steven's theater friends at the New Year's Eve concert after I'd gone home, and afterward they'd had their first big argument. "Do you know what Dominic calls me?" Noe had told me on the phone. "The bitch-monster from hell. He told me I was ruining Steven's life. And I'm like, 'You think I'm ruining his life? Who got him so drunk he tried to kill himself?'"

I hadn't realized that Noe had all but forbidden Steven to hang out with his old friends. I tried to sympathize with her like I always did when she was indignant about something, but the truth was I liked Steven's theater posse, and could understand why they'd be up in arms over the loss of him.

The first week back at school, two kids got expelled for drug dealing, another one got suspended for vandalism, and they had to stop the annual drunk-driving presentation twenty minutes in because the kids in the back row had smuggled in a bottle of vodka and were hollering so loudly you couldn't hear the speaker. We had a big meet coming up in gymnastics, and Ms. Bomtrauer gave us a speech about proper form, and that very same practice Vanessa Guittard fell off the uneven bars and broke her wrist.

Noe's New Year's resolution was to master something called a double aerial, which Sphinx had started to teach her at Gailer. The first time she didn't show up outside the Art room before lunch, Steven and I waited in the hall for fifteen minutes and then spent another fifteen searching the whole school for her. We found her in the gym, practicing on the beam, her backpack slumped against the wall.

"I'll meet you guys in the cafeteria," she panted, waving us back out like little mice.

Steven built her this whole beautiful tray with a sandwich and salad and an apple he somehow cut into heart-shaped slices, but when she finally showed up it was one minute before the bell, and all she did was chug the water, coo over the apple hearts, wipe the sweat off her forehead, and ask if anyone had gum.

Now that Noe wasn't coming to lunch consistently, Steven and I started hanging out in the bathrooms more. Our favorite one was the old-fashioned ladies' room near the computer labs. It had nice acoustics, and Steven liked to sing in there. Other times we'd go to the theater wing to hang out with Steven's friends and play card games. At first I couldn't make sense of the rules, but Steven's friends were patient, and pretty soon I started to get the hang of it.

One day, there were printed notices taped to all the bathroom doors informing students that anyone caught using the opposite sex's facilities would be subject to disciplinary action. Steven was called into the office. He came back enraged.

"This school is stuck in the Dark Ages," he said. "I try to end bathroom apartheid, and he treats me like a sex offender. 'You think you're pretty cute, McNeil. There's nothing cute about being a pervert.'"

He was quivering with the injustice and humiliation. His hands curled and uncurled on the table. I imagined Mr. Beek towering over him, spit spritzing out of his mouth as he lectured Steven about respect and behavior.

"The world isn't ready for pee parity," I said. "All the great revolutionaries were once considered perverts. It's kind of a rite of passage."

"Noe is horrified, of course," Steven continued, not ready to be consoled. "She thinks I should just back down. I think it was someone on the gym team who complained."

Even though I knew about their recent friction, his tone still struck me. It was the first time I had ever heard Steven express frustration with Noe, or really anything except pure and unfettered adulation.

"I'm sure she's on your side," I said, but later that day I saw them arguing by the far trees, and after that Steven stopped wearing the PEE SISTERS headband I'd made him for Christmas and which he'd been wearing every day since we got back from break.

I TRIED TO RIDE OUT THE craziness by cocooning into myself.

I ripped the CDs that Bob had lent me and loaded them onto my music player.

The Stone King has not been seen for two hundred years, but holds the land of Riddlespoon captive through a silent reign of terror. Can Rae of Riddlespoon free her people from his grasp?

"What are you listening to?" said Noe.

"Nothing."

"I was saying you should come to the YMCA on Sunday to work on your floor routine."

I turned down the volume. "Okay," I said.

The land of Riddlespoon used to be lush and verdant but was slowly turning to stone. The people were ruled by fear. Rae's mother, Genewren, lay paralyzed by the Stone King's curse, her once-strong limbs turned gray and cold.

"I will avenge her," Rae swore, and set out for the Doom Crags.

"Want to go to the Java Bean?" Noe said.

I pressed pause. "Sure."

The sidewalks were brown slush and flattened coffee cups. Shopping carts rattled unmoored across parking lots. Noe was wearing a pink-and-white knitted hat with a sparkly pom-pom on top, gloves to match. Her black coat was speckled with white lint.

When we got to the Java Bean, Steven's mom—Darla—was in line getting a cappuccino. Noe sang a hello and they traded air kisses while I stood awkwardly by the donut case.

"Hi there," Darla said, beaming down on me for a moment before turning back to ask Noe about her plans for spring break.

Her mouth was painted red and she was wearing a perfume you could smell all the way from the door, like a Mister Cookie outlet that pumps its odor of brownies and gingerbread a little too aggressively onto the sidewalk.

When Noe talked to Darla, she transformed. Gestures came out that I had never seen Noe do before, twirls of the wrist and rolls of the eye that mirrored Darla perfectly. They reminded me of the birds displaying their feathers in *Planet*

Earth: tweet tweet, flap flap. A bizarre kind of mating dance, it unsettled me to observe.

"Do you girls want a ride home?" Darla said.

"Would you?" Noe cooed, clapping her hands together as if a ten-block car ride was the greatest treat on earth.

Darla paid for our drinks and we walked out to her very clean, very new, very white SUV. The radio was tuned to a Christian rock station.

"Have you been to this nail salon yet?" Darla said, tapping her finger at a pink-and-silver storefront on the corner.

"No," Noe said. "We should *totally* go."

I put my earbuds on and started *Kingdom of Stones*.

82

THE NEXT DAY, AT LUNCHTIME, I sat on the gym floor and watched Noe practice.

She was beautiful on the beam, fluid as water. She looked like the ballerina in a jewelry box, her black hair drawn up to a bun on the top of her head, her eyes focused, the grip of her toes determined. I sat on the floor with my knees drawn up to my chest. I couldn't take my eyes away from her. Suddenly, the beam seemed so high and lonely it might as well have been a mountaintop. She turned lightly on the tips of her toes and my throat got so tight I thought I would cry. For some reason, I was remembering the time in tenth grade when Noe's dog had died. She'd cried on my bed and I hugged the soft, rumpled heap of her, and thought to myself that Noe was the person I loved most in the world.

As I was having that one memory, all sorts of other memories started flooding into me until it felt like I was seeing a replay of every heartbreaking moment in my entire life. Suddenly, I was in front of Scott's house again, alone in the cold twilight with a rock clenched in my hand.

"What?" Noe said.

I shook my head. When I blinked, the gym lights wobbled and swam.

"Are you sad?" Noe said, hopping down from the beam and walking over to crouch beside me. She ran her fingers through my hair like she always did when someone was crying or upset. It was one of her techniques. I bet she had read in a magazine that having your head scratched released endorphins or something. That was a very Noe thing to remember and put into practice.

She sat down cross-legged on the floor. Her fingernails were painted to match our gym leotards and she smelled different, more grown-up. I felt the secret tremble inside me like a butterfly beating its wings inside my hand, everything in me wanting to succumb to the comfort of *telling Noe*. So far I'd managed to avoid giving in to that particular temptation when it came to Scott.

"Poor thing," Noe said. "Are you regretting it?"

It took me a second to realize that Noe was talking about Maple Bay, and not about throwing the rock at Scott's window.

"No," I said truthfully.

"Are you sure?" Noe said. Her voice was all sympathy, her eyes their wide familiar brown. It was so *easy* to talk to Noe when she was like this, to climb into the warm fuzzy nest of that voice and feel yourself completely understood. No wonder she knew everyone's secrets. This time, however, I didn't have a secret to confess—at least, not the one Noe was fishing for.

"Of course," I said. "You think I secretly wanted a baby?"

Noe gave me a look. "Darla says all women want their babies unless they were, like, raped. It's a basic human instinct."

"I don't think so," I said stiffly.

If I was the clever, brave, and sassy girl in a high school drama, I would have said, *And besides, I didn't have a baby. I had a bundle of cells the size of a pencil eraser.* But I was too stricken to even think that, and it didn't occur to me until much later.

"It's not something you can think or not think," Noe said. "It's biology. Lots of women get really depressed afterward. One of the girls at Darla's church committed suicide last year."

I was used to hearing Noe hold forth about everything under the sun. I rarely had a reason to contradict her real or presumed authority. I shifted uncomfortably, feeling the muzzle trying to catch all my complicated words before they found their way out. The bell started ringing, and fourth-period gym class kids came through the gym doors in noisy clusters of two and three.

"Maybe she wouldn't have done that if people hadn't given her the idea that she was supposed to," I said to Noe as we stood up to put the beam away.

I should have said more. If I were Ava or one of Ava's runny-stockinged roommates, I could have given Noe this whole feminist education about all the reasons Darla was wrong, citing historical references and psychology papers. People got sad after making all kinds of decisions. It didn't mean the decisions were wrong. I wanted to tell Noe that sad and happy were things you lived with no matter which choices you made. That you couldn't stop them any more than you could stop the seasons from changing.

The gym was filling up with kids in white T-shirts and purple basketball shorts. My throat felt swollen and achy from sorting through all the things I could and could not say.

"I'm just worried about you," Noe said before we parted ways for our separate classes. "I want you to be okay."

She gave me a big, tight, Darla-scented hug. I nodded dumbly and walked away with my head reeling, wishing Noe had called me a slut or said I was going to hell. It would have been so easy to respond to an attack. This softer thing was more confusing. This feeling of bafflement at being so completely misunderstood. Even worse was the feeling that Noe and I no longer meshed in the same ways but still acted like we did.

I wanted Noe *back*, I thought with a pang. Noe of the spinning hug in the driveway, Noe of Camp Qualla Hoo Hoo. Noe before she became Little Miss Daughter-in-Law, before Sphinx Lacoeur. I missed that Noe. I missed myself. I missed us.

I thought about the night I came back from Northern, running out to meet her in the street. Were we even still ourselves back then, or had we already changed into these other people? Did we really mean it, or were we playing out our old rituals one last time, as a kindness, or a half-life, the way that light from a dying star continues to reach the earth for years after the star has burned out?

That afternoon, I went to the forest after school and trudged around the trails in the snow.

"You're pink," Mom said when I came home. "It's nice to see you outdoors."

I sank onto the couch and buried my head under a blanket.

Whatever was happening, I wouldn't call it *nice*.

THE SUNDAY BEFORE THE GYM MEET, I went to the YMCA and endured four and a half hours of Noe-directed torture. Halfway through, Ava called to see how I was doing. I went outside to talk with her, happy for an excuse to leave the mirrored dance room where Gym Bird Number Twelve was running through her floor routine for the fourth time while Noe made adjustments to her shoulders and hips and told her to aim for greater fluidity in all aspects of movement.

We talked for a while about Ava's friends and the theater festival she was helping put on.

"How are things with your mom?" Ava said.

"Pretty good."

"Pretty good?"

I looked at the sidewalk. Ever since Scott's house, I'd hardly been able to eat. It felt like the rock hadn't gone through his window, but was lodged in my stomach instead. I thought of Ava's room the day that she'd told me, the sadness that lived there.

"Ava?" I said. "I went to his house."

"Whose house?"

"Scott's. I broke his window." Something was clawing at my throat. In my stomach, the rock was burrowing itself as deep as it would go. "I saw him," I said. "He waved hello and said what a beautiful night it was."

"That's fucked up," Ava said.

"Yup."

From the sidewalk, I could hear the music Noe was playing for Hannah Garrity's floor routine one story above, muted against the window glass.

"Should I tell my mom?" I said. "About the window?"

"I don't know," Ava said. She sounded genuinely uncertain. "God, Annabeth. I don't know."

When I went back into the gym, Noe pounced on me. "There you are! Onto the mat, it's your turn. And take that sweater off."

She peeled it off me and tossed it onto the pile of sweaters and coats in the corner.

I shivered through the rest of practice. Someone had brought a box of clementines wrapped up in blue paper. I spent the last half hour sitting against the wall with a clementine cradled in my hands, its bright orange skin like a promise of warmth I could hold close to myself but never feel.

ON THE DRIVE HOME FROM THE YMCA, I told Noe I was thinking of going to see Bob again.

Noe pulled back, aghast. "Why?"

For some reason, I blushed. "I don't know," I said. "I mean, I do find it hard to eat sometimes. A lot of the time. When I'm feeling bad."

Noe dismissed this with a flick of her hand. "That's different. They can't make you go. Not unless your mom signed a form or something. It's illegal."

She kissed me on the cheek, a kiss that smelled vaguely sour. For some reason I thought about what Margot Dilforth had said. Maybe Noe was taking the fluidity thing even further than I realized. I shook the traitorous thought from my mind. Noe and I had been more or less back to normal since the *basic human instinct* conversation. At least, we made our normal jokes and had our normal interactions, although I could sense that something beneath the surface had changed.

Some friendships ended all at once and some were like Athenian ships, each part slowly replaced over the years until one day, even if you had never left the deck, you couldn't recognize it anymore. Lately when I talked to Noe I felt like one of the old people who came to the ice-cream shop year after year, even though the soul of the place had long ago drained out of it: they knew it wasn't the same anymore, but they simply didn't know where else to go.

"Get a good sleep," Noe said when we pulled up at my house. "Don't forget to shave your legs tomorrow morning or you'll look like a monkey. Bus leaves at seven sharp. No coffee unless you want your sweat to smell like the Java Bean." She winked at me. "Bye, doll."

GYM MEET, THE NEXT MORNING: FIRST the idling
school bus, then the half-hour ride that smelled of hair spray,
everyone brushing and braiding and squirting gel into their
hair and hunting in their gym bags for spare elastics. Music
playing on cell phones. Noe striding up and down the central
aisle with a clipboard, authoritative in her black-and-purple
tracksuit, attending to a thousand details whose significance
escaped me. I knew she was the team captain, but still it was
strange to see her like that, a Noe with no special allegiance to
me, who did not sit next to me at the seat I'd saved for us by the
window, who did not even alight there, but breezed past in a

whiff of Wintermint to confer with Ms. Bomtrauer about that morning's twentieth emergency.

I watched the town flash past outside the muddy bus window. Strip mall, gas station, then the highway. I wondered what would happen if someone opened the door of the bus and let us all fly away. Girls in spangled leotards hopping through the windows, pecking uselessly at the snow. Making eyes at themselves in toy mirrors while the winter wind froze first their spindly legs, then their blue feathers, then finally their tiny, twinkly hearts.

THE GYMNASIUM WHERE THE MEET WAS taking place was huge and busy, with multiple events going on at once. I had expected something more formal, with an audience and clapping, but in the junior levels it was more like waiting to take a driver's test: lots of standing in line and then a nervous two minutes on the equipment while the world continued to hum and churn around you. The real action was at the advanced events, where girls like Noe sailed through gravity-defying combinations of jumps and twists.

After my beam event (tippy two minutes scuttling up and down the plank) and my bars event (actually-kind-of-enjoyable two minutes bouncing and swinging eight feet above the ground) and my vault event (annoying: vault cleared, but only just), I went to the bathroom. The lights in there were buzzing quietly. The bathroom fixtures were even older than the ones at E. O. James, clammy faucets and an avocado-green paper towel dispenser right out of the seventies.

There was a girl retching in one of the toilet stalls. My first thought was that she was pregnant. I took an extralong time washing my hands, waiting for her to come out. Who knew? Maybe I could be her magic spirit friend. I still had that piece of birthday cake in my backpack. It was hard as a brick and dry as tinder. In a pinch, you could use it to light a campfire.

Hey, I would say. *If you need someone to talk to, I happen to have some experience in this domain.*

I dried my hands and waited quietly for another minute. Finally, the stall door swung open and Noe stepped out.

"Hey, doll," she said when she saw me. "Excited for your floor routine?"

She turned on the tap and swished her hands beneath the hot water. I watched her soap and rinse them, stunned into muteness. I had witnessed Noe doing this at least a dozen times since the Skittles incident in ninth grade. Now, for the first time, I saw it for what it was: Noe wasn't exempt. She wasn't different. She was a girl making herself puke in a toilet bowl.

I couldn't believe I'd never seen that before. I couldn't believe I'd told myself that *not* seeing it made me special and understanding, instead of simply a coward.

"Noe," I said. "I know what you're doing."

She kept on washing her hands, patient and businesslike. Her face in the mirror was undecipherable. She had put on lipstick and mascara so she wouldn't look "washed out" under the bright lights. Up close, the makeup made her look ghoulish, even vampiric.

"Emergency measures," Noe said. "My floor event got moved an hour earlier. No warning. If there's anything in your digestive tract, it can give you cramps." She patted my arm. "Trust me, I know what I'm talking about."

She was the same old Noe, amused and reassuring. *Poor dear* this and *poor darling* that. She pecked at the pins in her hair, rearranging them to fasten stray strands of hair out of the way.

"No," I said. "It's not emergency measures. It's crazy. Normal people don't make themselves throw up *ever*. You're hurting yourself."

I wanted her to soften, to yield, to let me gather her up and say, *Tell me everything*. Instead, Noe raised her eyebrows at me.

"Sphinx said not to eat a minimum of three hours before an event. Any less than that and it affects your fluidity. If they hadn't changed the stupid schedule, we wouldn't be having this conversation. I didn't work this hard all year just to let my floor routine get sabotaged."

"I don't think he meant for you to *throw up*."

"Actually, he said it was okay in emergency situations."

I hesitated. The light in the bathroom hummed. Noe put a hand on her hip. "Sphinx was an Olympic gymnast, Annabeth. Are you going to tell me he doesn't know what he's talking about?"

"He sounds like a dick."

"Can we table this?" said Noe. "I have to go stretch."

"Noe," I said. "You can talk to me about it. You don't have to be so *invulnerable* all the time."

"I need to go, Bethy. Seriously, don't worry."

She breezed past me and pushed the door open with both palms. I trailed after her, stunned and hangdog, and watched her curved shape disappear into the churning gym.

I didn't know what to do with myself until my next event, so I sat on some bleachers and took *How to Survive* out of my backpack. I was reading the part about poisonous plants when the coach, Ms. Bomtrauer, tapped me on the shoulder.

"Were you in the bathroom just now?" she said.

I nodded, surprised.

"Was Noe doing something she shouldn't be doing?"

I froze. I hadn't decided what to do yet. Instead of nodding or shaking my head, I made a slight shrug with my shoulders, as if to say, *Don't ask me, I don't want to be involved, Noe will kill me, I wasn't going to say anything, I don't know.*

Ms. Bomtrauer sighed and drummed her fingers on her clipboard. "That's all I needed to know."

She started to walk away.

"Ms. Bomtrauer?" I said.

"Mm-hmm?"

"The coach from Gailer told her—he said it was okay in emergencies."

Shit shit shit. I wasn't making it better at all. Ms. Bomtrauer frowned, and a deep furrow formed between her eyebrows. "What coach at Gailer?"

"Sphinx Lacoeur," I squeaked, regretting the moment I opened my stupid mouth.

"Hmph," she said, and walked away.

NOE WAS GOING TO KILL ME.

Noe was going to kill me.

Guilt bloomed inside me, hot and loud and red. If I hadn't gone to sit on the bleachers, if I hadn't been just *sitting* there, if I'd thought to compose an innocent face and say, *No . . .* in a surprised and wondering way. Noe would think I had sold her out, Noe would think I had betrayed her. As I watched her perform her floor routine, the guilt tossed and turned inside me until I felt like I was the one who was going to throw up. When would Ms. Bomtrauer confront her? Today? Later? I could feel the clock ticking, the moment approaching when a furious Noe would storm up to me and say, *Next time, how*

about you give me a little warning before you tell our coach that
Sphinx Lacoeur gave me a personal puking lesson?

I copied Noe and drank a bottle of water during lunchtime, rationing evenly so that it wouldn't slosh around inside me as she'd warned me that it could. I walked away from the spot on the floor where everyone was eating and practiced my switch jumps, my stomach panging with vindictive jabs of hunger. I wished I would faint or break my ankle so I could be driven away in an ambulance, the medical emergency rendering me saintly, making me innocent and lovable again. On one side of the gym, a photographer was taking team photographs. Flocks of gym birds posing for the camera flash.

A few minutes before my floor event, Noe walked over.

"Hey, squirrel. You look amazing," she said, holding me at arm's length to inspect me like a creation of hers that had turned out particularly well. "Did you eat?"

"Not yet."

"Good girl. We'll go to Subway after this, Alicia and Kaylee are going to need food too."

I gazed at her miserably. A bunch of girls came to join us on the bleachers where Noe and I were sitting. Soon Noe was chattering up a storm with them, analyzing the day's victories and defeats. The organizer called my name. I stood up to go to the floor. Noe tore herself away from the conversation for a moment.

"You look amazing, doll," she said again.

I grunted my thanks.

The music started. I sailed through the first cartwheel, the hip swivel and shoulder thrusts, aware of the fluorescent gym lights on my bare arms and legs. I'd wrestled my hair into a clumsy French braid and shellacked it in place with some of Kaylee Ito's gel. Now my own head smelled foreign to me, like a head out of a magazine.

I landed the second cartwheel smoothly and remembered to smile on the landing.

From the sidelines, a blinding flash. I glanced over and saw the photographer from the *Tribune* crouching there with his camera. He took another picture, *snap*, and grinned at me encouragingly. I threw myself into the round-offs. The next time I came up for air, I spied Ms. Bomtrauer approaching the bleachers where Noe was sitting. Step, step. I watched Ms. Bomtrauer summon Noe away from the rest of the girls and lead her to the wall to talk. Stag leap, stag leap. Noe's face changing from sunlight to storm clouds. Noe stalking back to the bleachers alone while Ms. Bomtrauer walked toward the vault area.

Half turn, stag leap, round-off. Noe sliding back into the front row. I came up from a somersault.

Bitch, Noe mouthed at me.

I faltered. The mat stretched out before me, blank and

impenetrable. I wished it would turn to water so I could dive under its surface and swim away. If this was a legend, I thought to myself, it *would* turn to water and I *would* swim away, and forever be known as the ghost mermaid who pulled hapless gymnasts into the mat to drown.

I turned, glimpsed Noe's face again, and this time I lost my grip on the smile. I could almost hear it dropping on the mat, a muffled *tink*. Lindsay Harris's tampon fell out in the middle of her beam routine, Noe had said. And Annabeth's smile slipped off her face and shattered into a hundred pieces. With the smile gone I lost control of my face, then my body, as if it had been the one thing pinning everything together. I thumped across the mat, feeling more and more angry with every slap of my feet.

Snap, went the camera. *Snap, snap.*

The music stopped. I swept my hands up, nodded tersely at the table of adjudicators, and walked off the floor, my face burning. I could feel Noe's eyes on the back of my head the whole way.

As I pushed through the changing room door, the next girl's routine was already starting. I glanced back and saw her land her first handstand, the confident way her arms swept through the air. There were moves, I realized, sequences in life you had to learn. A certain dance unlocked a certain door: a friendship, a romance, a progression from one level of things to the next. And while everyone else sailed through the steps, the best I could do was desperately ape them.

In the changing room, I was a girl with ten thousand reasons to hate herself. I sank onto the clammy wooden bench and held my face in my hands, feeling the reasons swarm over me like flies and cover me whole.

ON THE BUS RIDE HOME, NOE wouldn't even look at me. I hunched against the window. A hundred times, I tried to catch her eye—*It wasn't my fault, I swear, she asked* me, *I didn't tell her*—but Noe turned her face away. When we got to the school, Steven and Darla were waiting for Noe in the parking lot. They got out of Darla's huge car and waved. There was no nonawkward way of leaving the parking lot without saying hello to Steven, so I tromped behind Noe all the way to their car.

"How'd it go, honey?" Darla sang, sweeping Noe into her arms like a long-lost daughter. "DiMaggio's or Casa Italia? Your choice."

Just like that, Noe was Ms. Shiny-Brite again. "You're taking me out for dinner?" she squealed. "You guys are too sweet. Let's do DiMaggio's, I love their gnocchi."

I guess it was safe to eat again, provided Noe didn't need to do any double handsprings within the next three hours.

"Are you coming?" said Steven.

"I'm pretty wiped," I said.

"Please please please?"

"No thanks," I said glumly. "You guys have fun."

I said good-bye and walked away before Steven could wheedle me into coming. My muscles ached and I was hungry.

On the walk home, I kept scanning the sidewalks and the branches of the bare trees, as if I'd lost a precious necklace that might be wedged in a crack or snagged on a twig. I remembered the mixture of fear and certainty I'd felt when I confronted Noe in the bathroom, like a fantasy novel heroine uttering magic words to break a spell.

But that was where the analogy stopped. If I'd finally said the magic words, why had the treasure disappeared?

WHEN I GOT HOME, MOM COULD tell something was wrong.

"How was the gym meet?" she said.

"Fine."

"Win any ribbons?"

"A stupid photographer took my picture."

"Wow," said Mom mildly. "You're going to be famous."

I peeled off my hat and scarf and threw them onto the coat-rack. My winter coat was heavy and damp. I slithered out of it and dumped it onto a hook. The kitchen was warm and moist with cooking beans, a smell that was suddenly comforting. I leaned against the counter with my arms crossed, trembling with humiliation at the way Noe had stalked ahead of me to where Darla and Steven were waiting without even acknowledging that I was there.

"What are you cooking?" I said.

"Vegetarian chili."

"It smells good."

"Thanks."

"Can I chop something?"

"How about some onions?"

She made room for me at the counter. I took an onion from the wooden bowl and peeled off the papery yellow skin. Mom was using the good knife, so I poked around in the drawer until I found one that was almost as sharp.

"Do you want to invite Noe over for dinner?" Mom said.

"She went to a restaurant with her boyfriend and his mom."

"Aha," said Mom. "I was wondering why she'd been so scarce around here. I haven't seen her in months."

We peeled and chopped. It had been a long time, I realized, since I'd confided in Mom about anything. The last time was when my seventh-grade best friend, Emily Lincoln, had two birthday parties, a boring one with me and Carly Ocean and Eliza Grinette, and a fun one with her cool friends where there was dancing and making out and somebody brought a beer. I couldn't believe I'd been assigned to the "boring friend" category, lumped in with *Carly Ocean*. Mom had taken me on a walk in the woods and listened to me wail, and afterward we'd picked up Nan and gone out for French fries at Dick's Chips and everything had started to feel okay. Ever since Ava told me about Scott, I'd stopped unpouring myself to Mom, like my problems were silly compared to what she'd been through. Like I owed it to her to be perfect so she wouldn't have any more reasons to regret me.

Now the knife I was holding blurred before my eyes. I set it down.

"I thought we were going to be friends forever," I burst. "I care about her so much. But it's like we're not *communicating* anymore."

"You're still pretty disappointed about the roommate thing, aren't you?" said Mom.

"Not as much since I visited Ava," I said. "But yeah. It's like she decided to become this whole different person, but I'm not allowed to become a different person too."

"People are like trees," said Mom. "They need one kind of food when they're seedlings, and a different kind of food once they've been growing for a few years. Maybe you and Noe needed each other in ninth grade in a way you don't need each other now."

I imagined myself as a scrawny sapling, the fertilizer of Noe slowly being withdrawn, the wooden stakes pulled up.

"You and Pauline stayed friends," I said.

"Pauline and I didn't *become* friends until we were in college."

"Really?"

She smoothed the hair off my forehead, a gesture I hadn't allowed her to do in years. "Annabeth, honey, life keeps on changing. You don't get one chance at friendship, or one chance at love. Things die. Things grow. It's hard to see that when you've only been around for seventeen years, and you've only ever had one of everything, but it's true."

"I just wish we could do it without turning into enemies."

"Well," Mom sighed. "That's the hard part."

We picked up our knives and started chopping again, and soon it was time to eat.

I HAD HOPED THAT NOE WOULD come around. But the next day in English, she sat down and opened her book without so much as a glance in my direction.

Are you still mad? I wrote on a piece of paper I slipped onto her desk. She pushed it back without looking at it.

For the rest of class, I felt as queasy as the time my cousin Max dared me to swallow a raw egg. When the bell rang, Noe picked up her backpack and stalked out. I dawdled, putting away my notebook and pens, the raw egg feeling creeping from my stomach to my throat.

I left a note in Noe's locker—*Talk to me!*—and hurried away. In the hallway, Mr. Beek was making Jamie Appleton pick up every single piece of trash from a garbage bin somebody had knocked over. Outside the window and across the street, the Burger King was advertising Double Bacon Cheeseburgers. I thought I glimpsed the nutritionist coming out the door, but it could have been some other big, sad person with their head bent over a paper bag.

91

THE NEXT MORNING, STEVEN PESTERED ME all through Art. "Noe won't tell me what happened. Should I be afraid?"

"It's not about you," I said. "She's mad at me."

"Why?"

Steven's cheeks were always red in the winter, like apples in snow.

"Have you figured out her food thing yet?" I said.

"I have suspicions," Steven said. "I've been badgering her. With reason, it appears?"

I put my head on the table. I couldn't even summon the energy to moan. Deep inside me, the place where Noe lived was aching and aching.

"You're going to think I'm a horrible friend," I said.

"Why?" said Steven. "Did you trick her into eating foie gras?"

"I caught her throwing up. And I told her she should stop. And then Ms. Bomtrauer asked me if I'd seen Noe doing it, and I was too surprised to lie."

"That doesn't make you a horrible friend," said Steven.

"But I've known for four years. And it was the first time I said anything."

"I'll talk to her," Steven said.

"You shouldn't," I said. "It will only make things worse."

The classroom smelled like paint, and paint remover. I wondered how many hours were left until graduation.

92

I DIDN'T WANT TO GO TO gymnastics practice, but I was afraid that flaking would make Noe even madder. Ms. Bomtrauer led us through a warm-up and started us on our usual rotation around the beam, bars, vault, and floor. I tried to act normal, but it felt like Noe was watching me the whole time.

"Toes," shouted Noe from across the gym, and I yelped, "Sorry," landing my pivot leap flat on my feet.

I tried to laugh it off—maximum-security gymnast and all that—but my face flooded with heat.

"You're so curled up," Noe said irritably. "Shoulders back."

"They don't *go* that far back," I said.

When Noe was like this, I couldn't meet her eyes. If I was ink, she was bleach. It burned to look at her, to see my own leaky blackness reflected in her expression, when all I wanted was for things to be tidy and clear. I worked on my pivot leap for the rest of practice, pointing my toes until they ached, forcing my shoulders into shapes that would never, ever look like the gentle ripple they were supposed to.

There was something strange in the air. Everyone was acting weird. I felt the other girls' eyes prickling on me as I teetered up and down the balance beam. At first I wrote it off to the drama of the gym meet. *Annabeth told Ms. Bomtrauer that Sphinx Lacoeur brainwashed Noe and it isn't even true.*

But as practice went on, the prickling got worse and worse. People were definitely looking at me. I saw them out of the corner of my eye. The queasy feeling came back. I moved from the beam to the uneven bars, trying to ignore it, but it only got stronger and stronger. I stopped mid-spin and dropped down from the bars, clutching my stomach as if to indicate that I had a cramp. As I limped toward the water fountain, I could feel the eyes of the entire team on me and hear whispers throughout the gym. I realized with a sickening tightness in my stomach that they had been told something. By the time I had made it the three hundred feet to the door, I *knew.*

I picked up my gym bag. Someone had scrawled *babykiller* on the side in permanent marker.

I pushed through the heavy doors and into the yellow hallway.

I wanted to crawl into a tunnel made of dirt and stones and stay there until everyone I knew had grown old and died and there wasn't anyone left to look at me like that anymore.

THE WALK BACK TO MY HOUSE: rattled and uncomprehending, close to tears.

Overhead, yellow leaves flapped in the treetops. A crow cawed. I bent mid-stride and scooped up a piece of gravel from the road and put it in my mouth and sucked until the top of my mouth had turned to blood.

94

THE NEXT MORNING, I PACKED MY backpack slowly, deliberately, as if packing for a desert island. Peanuts, fresh water, textbooks, pens. *How to Survive.* I still hadn't read the poem Loren had sent me, or written back to his email. I printed the poem, folded it in half, and stuck it between the chapters on shelter and navigation. Something told me I was going to have lots of time to read for the rest of the year.

I combed my hair and brushed my teeth.

"Your gym coach called," Mom said when I went downstairs. "Were you sick yesterday?"

She was wearing her No Frills uniform, a yellow apron over a white blouse. For a second, I considered playing the get-out-of-school card. But the truth was, I was feeling abundantly healthy. And I knew that to hide now would only make things worse.

"Sick of gymnastics," I said. "You were right. It's been horrible. Noe's on my case all the time and everyone cares too much about their stupid hair and makeup and I just want to kick something."

The fridge hummed. Mom picked up her purse. "Just make sure to get that deposit back for the leotard," she sighed.

IF YOU COME TO MY SCHOOL in late January, you will inevitably wonder why the building hasn't been condemned as a health hazard.

The classrooms in which the heaters work are warm and damp, like incubators for mold.

The classrooms in which the heaters don't work are so cold you can't hold a pencil.

The couches in the back corner of the library are polka-dotted with gum and tobacco juice and the crusty stains of bodily fluids that will not be cleaned off until next fall.

The floors are covered in a brown layer of slush that nobody ever mops up. You can literally slide to your classes.

All these conditions serve to make the students bored and aggressive and prone to gossip.

Sometimes it feels like nobody gets out of here without a broken bone or two.

96

THE FIRST DAY WITHOUT NOE WAS THE hardest. For the most part, I avoided eye contact with anyone in our year, and kept my ears firmly plugged with earbuds at all times during which it wouldn't earn me a detention to do so. I started *Kingdom of Stones* again from the beginning. It was comforting to hear about Rae as a young villager again, before she has any of her harrowing adventures. I wished I could go back to Book One of my own life, when all was good and peaceful in Riddlespoon and the Stone King hadn't yet sown his death-seeds through the land.

My campaign of avoidance wasn't entirely successful.

Margot Dilforth: "Is it true that you're pregnant?"

Me: "No."

Margot Dilforth: "That's what everyone's saying."

Something about her reminded me of a goat. In *Kingdom of Stones*, she would be Penny-foo, the annoying milkmaid. I remembered what Margot was like in middle school, an earnest girl with long braids. Always at the edge of things, trying to buy her way into the center by impressing people with scandalous information.

Margot Dilforth: "Are you and Oliver getting married?"

Me: "Not that I know of."

Margot Dilforth (scratching her long, freckly nose): "I heard you are."

Steven was away on a theater trip that day. In Art, I had to sit alone. I wanted to call him, but suddenly our little triangle had gotten very messy. Steven was wrong. It wasn't as simple as being friends instead of friends-by-association. He was *dating* the association, and right now, the association hated my guts.

I planned all my routes to avoid intersecting with Noe, but I came across her by accident, in a basement hallway, surrounded by a feathery knot of gym birds. There was nowhere to hide. Nobody to hide behind. I stood tall and walked past them at a slow, normal, nothing-is-wrong pace while everything in me longed to run.

Noe was crying. The gym birds were comforting her.

Nobody looked at me while I walked past.

91

SCHOOL WAS LONELY. WORDLESSLY, WITH NO further discussion or negotiation, Noe and I ceased to be, the way a dry leaf detaches itself from the branch and spirals silently toward the ground. The soccer fields outside the school building were messy expanses of trampled ice. The classrooms smelled like wet coats. In Art, Steven and I whittled totem poles out of our pencils. We named the ancient paper cutter on the counter of the art morgue Ernestine.

"Ernestine looks lonely today," Steven would say, and we would take turns getting up to pet her.

"Ernestine is hungry," I'd say, and we'd find excuses to chop some paper up with her heavy old blade.

In the hallways, posters for the Valentine's Day ball. The Senior Leaders set up tables outside the cafeteria selling tickets. You couldn't walk in for lunch without them shaking their bags of Hershey's Kisses at you.

"Bought your tickets for the ball?" they'd shout like hawkers outside a football stadium (or "Hey! You like balls?" if they were guys). They made you feel like crap if you walked past without stopping, like you were the one being rude. They did it to everyone, even the nervous freshmen, especially the nervous freshmen. Like all the other nervous people, I scuttled past with my eyes averted, muttering, "No thanks."

"Why not?" they'd call after me, as if to prolong the humiliation by extracting a detailed explanation.

I pushed my earbuds deeper into my ears and kept walking.

At the lockers across the hall from mine, Noe and Dulcie Simmonds made plans: dress shopping, hair and makeup, restaurant selection, what Steven and Mark would wear. They had an entire shared notebook full of Valentine's Ball to-do lists and clippings from hairstyle magazines. Steven's mom was taking them to her manicurist, then for something called a radiant light treatment at the Twin Oaks Spa.

"What about my radiant light treatment?" said Steven.

"*You* will be getting a car wash," Noe said.

"Annabeth," called Steven. "Are you in on this?"

He had been trying to get Noe and me to make up for the

past two weeks. It was a complicated dance, and I could tell it was wearing him out. I'd seen them arguing again, and I'd hurried past with my head hunched, wishing he would just do as I'd pleaded and enjoy the rest of the year without worrying about me. I'd been doing my best to keep my distance outside Art so as to not mess things up for him, but he wasn't making it easy.

Noe ignored Steven and kept chatting with Dulcie. I shook my head. He gazed at me forlornly. "You two," he said, to no one in particular.

98

I HAD TOLD MYSELF I WOULDN'T miss Noe, that I would simply ignore her for the rest of the year. But there was a part of my brain where Noe lived, like a program I couldn't figure out how to delete from my phone. Now that we weren't speaking anymore, it played all the time. When I took a bite of my sandwich, I could hear Noe saying, *Somebody's hungry today.* When Ava called to see how I was doing, Noe said, *How are you even talking to that freak?* When I caught myself feeling happy at odd moments, Noe said, *Aren't you even a little ashamed?*

She lived inside me as a critical voice, telling me what a failure I was and how undeserving of love. Every time I passed her in the hall, or glanced at her accidentally in English, something inside me sent up a guilty flare. I wrapped my sandwich in a napkin. I deleted the email I was mentally composing to Loren Wilder. I pulled the sleeves of my sweater over my hands.

When I saw her, a sick shiver happened in the quease of my stomach. She had become frightening to me. I was hyperaware of her, the way you can't stop thinking about a spider in your room. Even when I wasn't looking directly at her, I could *sense* her, two rows behind me in the auditorium, twenty feet ahead of me in the hall. My ears pricked to every syllable of her voice laughing with other girls. I detected her every footfall, every toss of her oily black hair.

She cornered me in the hall one day.

"I just want you to know that it wasn't me who wrote that thing on your bag," she said. "It was Kaylee."

Noe's hair smelled like pomegranate. Her hands were calloused from the vault. It had been weeks since we'd stood this close to one another, or spoken face-to-face. I'd been building up this whole demonic story about her—Noe was controlling, Noe was cruel, Noe had never been my friend, and she didn't really love Steven either—but standing near her, smelling her smell, I couldn't see her as a demon anymore, even though I wanted to. What I did see: a girl who was just as scared as I was, and hurting just as much.

Noe, I wanted to say. *I see you. I can see you again. Can you see me?*

But I didn't say anything. I was too stunned.

We stood in the hall, people flowing past us like water. It seemed like the kind of moment in which we might have forgiven each other, in which two people with a history of friendship might reasonably be expected to forgive each other. I could see the moment of forgiveness blowing past us like a flowered dress tumbling in the wind on the side of the highway. Either of us could have said, *Pull over and grab it!* But neither of us did.

Noe turned. I adjusted my backpack with shaky hands and walked away.

99

AFTER THAT I STARTED SPENDING LUNCH in the sound booth. The auditorium was always empty these days; even Steven didn't think to look for me there. I read *How to Survive* and played with the lights, blending greens and blues and purples on the empty stage.

Other times I just sat in the dark and didn't move until it was time to go home.

100

IN ART, MR. LIM GAVE ME back my jar of stones with a yellow sticky note with a big letter *R* for Redo. I wished he would just give me a zero, since the assignment was now almost five months late.

The jar of stones sat on my desk all through class. People looked at it, and looked at me, and my neck prickled with self-consciousness. Midway through class, Steven slipped a note across the table.

Dear A, the note said.

Morgue Master Lim is clearly a dilettante. The substitution of stones for fruit speaks volumes. Instead of something sweet and ripe, something cold and hard. The stones/secrets are sealed inside her; the smooth glass surface of the jar belies the disordered rubble within, barely keeping it at bay.

The juxtaposition of the two pieces, furthermore, is striking. The first, dry twigs, are fruitless and bare. The second piece is full to the brim, but still manages to speak of hunger. She is trying to nourish herself with food only fit for a ghost. I would be worried about her, too.

Regards,

Steven McNeil

I slipped out of class as soon as the bell rang, in what had become my daily escape routine. Steven didn't come after me, but the note burned in my pocket for the rest of the day.

On the radio, blizzard warnings.

At home, bags of driveway salt.

The local paper showed a picture of Noe in the sports section, leaping over a vault to nowhere. LOCAL GYMNAST SOARS TO NEW HEIGHTS.

I wondered if Kaylee Ito had always hated me.

101

THAT NIGHT I WENT FOR A walk past the half-built houses near Lorian Woods, their harsh geometry softened by snow. I felt sorry for them. They looked hungry, hungry and dumb, like tourists who hadn't come dressed for the weather. I walked into the woods and looked at the way the branches fractured the sky. I put my hand on a tree's bark and felt a quiet current of friendship there.

Maybe it wasn't too late for me to freeze in a snowbank. It sounded almost dreamy, almost pleasant.

"Annabeth's wandered out and frozen," they'd say. "It's very sad."

I walked to the edge of the woods and lay in a snowbank. I

looked at the stars and remembered being younger.

Sometimes, Dad was the moon. Sometimes he was the man on the radio singing "Brown Eyed Girl." Sometimes he was the truehearted woodsman in *Little Red Riding Hood*, about to stride in with his ax to claim me. On one too-fast hike with Mom, the snacks all gone and the winter sunlight waning, I let her get farther ahead of me than ever before. I'd left the trail and sat down under a tree, pulling my hood up and cinching my jacket more tightly around my waist and neck. Before long, I knew, he would come striding through the woods in tall leather boots and a green feathered cap (he was Robin Hood, sometimes) and carry me on his shoulders all the way to a sturdy log cabin with cookies on the table and a tiny orange kitten like the one in my fantasies that Mom would never let me have. *Say hello to Stallion*, Dad would say, pouring the purring animal into my arms (How did he know her name would be Stallion?). *She's yours.*

Instead the sky had darkened and the temperature dropped. After several hours—five minutes, maybe—I heard Mom calling my name, and glimpsed her coming down the trail. In spite of myself I'd leaped up and shouted, "I'm here," my five-year-old's resolve wavering at the sight of her familiar sweater and hat. She scooped me up and hoisted me onto her back, and within a few minutes I was lulled to sleep by the steady up-down jostle of her stride. That night was pizza-and-ice-cream at Uncle Dylan's house, and a turn on my cousin Max's new computer game. They were always especially nice to me, Uncle Dylan and Aunt Monique and Nan and the cousins. By the time Mom put me to bed, I'd forgotten about the orange kitten for a while.

Overhead, the ice-encrusted branches rattled in the breeze, sending down a flurry of snow. For a long time now, there had been no benevolent moon-spirit watching over me, no radio-father singing "Brown Eyed Girl," and the man in the forest was a smirking boy I must be prepared to fight hand-to-hand and, if necessary, kill.

How were you supposed to move on from something like that?

I lay in the snowbank and waited to sleep. Eventually I got up and walked back home.

What's that Tom Waits song? "The Ocean Doesn't Want Me Today."

The snowbank didn't want me. There was no use fighting. I don't believe everything I hear in songs, but when you lie in a snowbank for an hour without falling asleep, the message is pretty clear.

IN DRAMA, WE HAD A NEW teacher, Ms. Hoffstadter, who was on loan from some school in England. I guess teachers can go on exchange too. She wore bloodred pants and a white blouse, and earrings made of slender purple feathers. For the first couple of weeks she had us doing drama exercises, which were pretty okay because they were largely silent—pretend you are carrying a staggering weight on your back, pretend you are dragging your weight across the floor, pretend you are being crushed beneath it. I didn't have to talk to anyone, just walk around in circles with these invisible torments. She had us memorize parts in a Lillian Hellman scene, then put on the scene without speaking.

"Words are the last layer," she said. "The tip of the iceberg. Ninety-nine percent of theater takes place in the body."

We pulled our invisible weights around, and moved them from shoulder to shoulder, and put them down and walked away and came back and picked them up exactly where we had left them. At the end of each class, Ms. Hoffstadter made us stack our weights neatly against one wall.

One day, I got so tired from dragging my weight around the gritty floor that I fainted. I don't know how it happened. It was a gray day. I was cold all the way through. I had been cold for days. The cold was inside my skull. I couldn't knock it out or melt it. That morning I'd taken a hot shower, but the cold was still there when I got out. My arms got all goose-bumpy under my sweater. You know when you put something in the oven but forget to turn it on, then you go to check it and it's still frozen? My goose-bumpy arms were like that. Still frozen, even though I'd been inside the school building all day.

We were doing our usual warm-up with our invisible weights, and I felt like I was going to sneeze, and then I woke up with my cheek on the floor and seven or eight people standing over me. Ms. Hoffstadter dispatched a girl named Win to walk me to the nurse's office. I hadn't realized I had a fever. Win felt my forehead while we were walking down the hall.

I drank the burning juice the nurse gave me and sat in a chair with a fleece blanket that smelled like cupboard and waited for my mom to come.

She stroked my forehead on the car ride home. She had the radio on, some talk show with a scientist. I fell asleep but didn't realize it, and the talk show kept going in my dream.

"Butterflies burrow underground in the winter," the scientist was saying. "Their dens are often six feet deep."

My brain pawed through these secret caches of butterflies like a hungry raccoon. Noe and I should go digging for them, said my dream-brain.

"Here we are, Annabean," Mom was saying. She undid my seat belt for me, *click*.

She hadn't called me Annabean in years. Maybe she called me that all the time, and I didn't notice.

I lay on the couch and she tucked me in with blankets and gave me a candy for my throat. It burned a hole in my cheek. I spat it into a tissue. The clock on the DVD player said 10:11 a.m., which seemed too early to be taking a nap.

Mom was in the kitchen making tea. I fell asleep before the tab on the kettle clicked up.

103

I WAS SICK FOR FIVE DAYS, hot all the way through except when I stood up or moved, in which case the cold reasserted itself in queasy flashes. I wore a hat inside the house, and thick socks. When I was sleeping, I thought I was hiking. Every time I woke up, confusion: where were the snow and the pine trees? Then I'd fall asleep again—*Ah, there they are.* Sometimes I'd get up and chug half a box of orange juice and hurry back to the couch so I could be on my hike again. The hike made sense. The hike had clear parameters and a clear sense of momentum. The hike was all body. It had nothing to do with words. I wished I could turn all my problems into sacks of stones I only had to carry around, into mountains I only had to wear my legs out climbing. I was tired of trying to think my way through life, of having to explain and justify and make myself acceptable to the world. I wanted to lift, to drag, to climb, to smash, to bushwhack.

Maybe it wasn't too late to have a lobotomy and finish my life as the Incredible Hulk, pure muscle. I could follow directions. I'd make a great firefighter, charging in with my hose. Maybe I should join the army. I wouldn't have to decide what to wear, or what to eat, or who to say hi to or not say hi to in the hall. Uncle Dylan was always hassling Max to sign up. Maybe I'd ask him about it, next time we went over for dinner.

I fell in and out of these thoughts, in and out, in and out. I dreamed I had already joined the army, and had a narrow gray bed in a cell like a nun's. I dreamed Noe and I were best friends.

Mom read in the living room. Cars hummed up and down the street. I felt like a drop of blood, all surface tension. I felt like the deer heart the hunter presented to the evil stepmother instead of Snow White's. I would always be the flea-bitten deer whose heart gets chopped out to save Snow White, I thought to myself. And maybe that was okay. Maybe that was worth it. In my dreams, I saved an old lady from a bathroom stall again and again.

I shivered and shivered. Mom came and went from work.

Wrapped up on the couch with a fever, exempt from all duties of life. Was there anywhere safer in the world?

104

ON THE FIFTH DAY MOM CAME home from work early. I was frozen solid. Several times I told myself to greet her, but somehow I ended up asleep before the "Hi, Mom" came out. I remembered and forgot and fell asleep, woke, remembered, forgot, until she woke me herself, lowering herself to the floor beside me.

"Annabeth," she said. "I think you should try to sit up for a while."

I shifted on the couch. Every time I moved, snow packed into the newly exposed parts of my body. I sat up with difficulty, my teeth chattering.

Mom was holding a big envelope. "Look what came," she said.

She handed it to me. The front of the envelope said CON-GRATULATIONS. The return address said NORTHERN UNIVERSITY.

I wept while Mom called Nan and Uncle Dylan. I wept while she called Pauline to tell her the news. I wept until I felt her arms lift me up and carry me, too easily, to bed.

105

WHEN I WENT BACK TO SCHOOL on Monday, grass was showing through the snow in damp green patches. The sun looked like a scrambled egg. At some point in the week I was gone, the school had received the projectors that were supposed to arrive in September as part of a Technology in the Classrooms grant. In class, the teachers mostly fussed with them while we sat bathed in cancerous blue light.

Sphinx Lacoeur had gotten fired, or almost fired, after Ms. Bomtrauer had called Gailer College to complain about the questionable health advice he was giving impressionable young gymnasts—I never got the whole story. The gym birds were up in arms over the injustice. You could see them twittering and puffing in the halls, skinny hips cocked, arms folded.

Noe had started to wear a tiny gold cross on a fine chain. You could barely make out its glimmer around her neck. She carried around a thick book called *Foucault's Pendulum* and a pink travel mug with GAILER COLLEGE embossed on the side.

Margot Dilforth had shocked everyone by making out with another girl at a St. Patrick's Day party. Now they were walking around the halls arm in arm. I had never seen Margot Dilforth looking radiant before. I wouldn't have thought it was possible. Now she glowed.

At lunch, I went to the nutritionist's office, knocked, and walked in. He was knitting a green-and-white dog sweater and had a new audiobook playing. I saw the CD case on his desk: *Entering Mist.*

The way to Master Tung's house was up the twelve-peaked mountain . . .

Bob didn't bother to scramble for the stop button. He set his knitting down, leaned forward, and gently clicked the player off.

"Annabeth," he said. "What a surprise."

I tossed a small blue notebook onto his desk and plunked myself onto the creaky plastic chair.

"I was thinking we could start over," I said.

He picked up the notebook and flipped through it. As he read through the columns, he began to sit up straighter. When he looked back at me, there was something like confidence in his face. He cleared his throat and adjusted the collar on his shirt.

"So, Annabeth. How long have you had trouble eating?" he said.

106

I WASN'T TRYING TO STARVE MYSELF. I was just too sad to eat.

Bob said that happened sometimes, when people got stressed.

He said the main thing was learning to feel good again.

"What would make you feel good?" he said.

I didn't have an answer for that, so mostly we ate Cheez-Its and listened to *Entering Mist*.

107

I STARTED GOING BY BOB'S OFFICE now and then when I got hungry. He kept a cardboard box full of trail mix packets outside the door. I felt like a bird visiting a bird feeder throughout the winter. I started making detours to go past the box throughout the day. Sometimes I was afraid it would be empty, but it never was. I tore into the packets as I hurried away, and inhaled the nuts and seeds so fast I couldn't taste them.

108

ONE DAY, STEVEN CAUGHT ME PAWING through the trail mix box. I jerked away guiltily. We were the only two people in the hall.

"Annabeth," he said, and I bolted like a deer, unable to make myself look back.

After that, there were sometimes chocolate éclairs in the box, and sometimes chili garlic peanuts, and sometimes neatly wrapped bowls of spinach-mushroom ravioli.

Somehow, I was always able to eat the things that came from Steven, as if the charm of friendship was the one thing powerful enough to overcome the curse of the Stone King.

109

SPRING BREAK WAS COMING UP. STEVEN was
going to Connecticut with his mom to visit his dying grandpa.
In Art, I made a PEE SISTERS badge for him and sewed it into
the sleeve of his sweater, just above the wrist. When he saw
what I had done, he got to work on a badge for me. When we
walked out, we both had neon-green hearts hidden under our
cuffs. Before splitting up at the end of the hall, I gave him a big
hug.

"Take good care of your grandpa," I said, before slipping
away.

110

THE LAST TIME I HUNG OUT in Bob's office before
the break, we got to the part in *Entering Mist* where Wu goes
to stay with a band of forest monks who rely on magical tree
energy to stay alive. The tree energy is called "nwiffer," and the
monks absorb it by being somewhere green.

When we got to that part in the audiobook, I blurted, "I
used to be like that."

"Like what?" said Bob.

"Full of nwiffer."

As I said it, I remembered a time before the monster. The
feeling started in my toes and spread upward, a pale green leaping. I remembered the hush of wind in the treetops, and the

striking red of Mom's hat against the leaves. I remembered gazing at the mirror in my vain moments, so pleased with myself. So certain of my own valor. So *certain*.

Bob said that my task for spring break was to get some nwiffer, and if I happened to eat more that would be a bonus.

I spent the week walking all the old trails, letting the green feeling spread from my toes to my ankles to my knees. I sat by the river and listened to the water until my body seemed to disappear in the sound. I thought about everything that had happened that year, from the first morning of school, to the moment Oliver and I began to kiss in the orchid house, to the abortion, to the gym meet, and everything in between. As the memories rose to my mind, they seemed to flow through me and disappear with each new swirl in the river. Maybe this was what life was, just this: one big ripple. I could live with that. I could let it go on and on.

In the evenings, Mom and I pored over the course catalog that Northern had sent, and talked on the phone with Ava and Pauline. Mom was thinking about going back to school to be a paramedic; one day her own fat envelope came in the mail, and we pored over that instead.

ON THE FIRST DAY BACK FROM spring break, Steven came to Art wearing a crown of daisies in his hair, and a chain of tiny bells around his ankle that he'd found on the street.

"I just want to *be* springtime," he said to me. "Don't you?"

He seemed floatier than usual, not quite okay. He wouldn't answer my questions about his grandpa. Finally, I dragged him to the bathroom and sat him down on the edge of the sink.

"Steven," I said. "What's going on?"

"Oh, nothing," he sang, and then he dropped his head onto my shoulder and began to weep.

112

SPRING BREAK HAD BEEN A DISASTER.

On his second day in Connecticut, Noe had chatted him, saying all this stuff about how *concerned* she and Darla were about Steven going off to NYU, and encouraging him to stay closer to home.

"Concerned why?" I said.

"I'm depressed," he said. "Remember? If Noe's not there to monitor me, I could tumble into a downward spiral and end up like my uncle."

"What's wrong with your uncle?"

"He's a writer. He smokes pot. He wears pretty shoes."

"He sounds cool."

"He *is*."

After an hour and a half of discussing Steven's "depression," she'd finally gotten to the point: she'd gone for a walk with Senior Leader Alex and discovered the true meaning of romance.

Steven took out his phone and showed me the chat transcript. I cringed, skimming the long exchange.

we haven't really been together since new years, Noe had said.

what do you mean? Steven had said.

what about the valentines ball?

and that day we played chess in the library?

and all the notes?

you spent half the valentines thing at margot and dominic's table

i hardly even saw you

and we haven't kissed since rhiannon's party

we've hardly had lunch together since last semester

i figured we'd reverted

?!?!?!

"reverted"

?

i thought it was mutual

i didn't think it needed some big discussion

we said "i love you."

you don't revert from "i love you" without a big discussion
that's what "i love you" means

Steven's tears and snot were soaking into my sweater. The daisies in his hair were getting crushed, the white petals curling in. I pulled the vial of lavender oil out of my pocket and quietly anointed him on the wrists, forehead, and heart, thinking that the mysterious thing about love is that you don't have to know what you're doing in order to do it exactly right.

I THOUGHT THAT STEVEN WOULD BE shattered by
the sight of Noe and Alex holding hands in the hall and studying together in the library. Already, the gym birds were chirping
about them like they were the Couple of the Year. Every minute I wasn't beside Steven, I was worrying about him. But after
a few days, he actually seemed happier. There was a spring in
his step, and a freshness to the way he clicked open his pencil
box to draw. At lunch, he dragged me to a table where Win
from my drama class was sitting.

"You two should be friends," he said. "Win, Annabeth.
Annabeth, Win. You should do your one-act play together."

Win and I exchanged glances and mutually rolled our eyes

as if to say, *Crazy old Steven McNeil.*

"I'm serious," said Steven. "You're perfect for each other. You're both insanely smart, you both love trees. You should write a play together. I demand it."

"What is this, Steven, your last will and testament?" joked Win.

He said nothing, but put one of his hands on Win's and one on mine and piled the hands together.

"Be friends," he said. "Sit together at lunch."

The cafeteria rattled around us. Sun poured through the window, the weak sun of almost-spring, slung low in the tree-tops. All I knew was I was happy to see Steven okay.

For the next few days, Steven glowed brighter than ever. He shined his shoes. They glowed too. They looked like Magic 8 Balls. When we passed each other in the hall, he would slip his arm through mine and twirl me around. Or he would be singing a Gershwin song, and he would smile and widen his eyes at me without breaking pace. He didn't seem like a boy who had just had his heart broken. He seemed like a boy in love. After he'd cried on my shoulder in the bathroom, I'd started to plan a whole consoling afternoon. I had an idea that we would skip art class and drink gin and smoke cigars and ride the SkyTram over the river. That seemed like a good post-breakup thing to do, a good distraction.

But Steven didn't seem like he needed distraction. His resilience threw me off. I didn't know how to broach the subject of the breakup with him.

At our newly founded lunch table, he seemed almost manic, piling up the salt and pepper shakers into towers twenty shakers tall. He talked incessantly, comic prattle about books and teachers and food and theater and the tutor his parents had hired to stop him from failing math. He didn't mention Noe at all. It was like he had forgotten her, or was immune to her.

I couldn't imagine being immune to Noe.

Even now, several weeks after the incident, I still winced when I passed her in the hall. I still felt a stab in my heart when my eyes fell on one of the ten thousand tokens of her that cluttered my desk and my bedroom walls, or when I overheard other girls making plans to go to Paris, or open funny restaurants together, or get matching tattoos on the day after graduation. It felt like a certain key bone in my skeletal system had been deleted, and I was still learning how to walk without it.

Or maybe I'd been limping all along, and this was just what it felt like to find my stride.

114

WIN AND I STARTED SMILING AT each other in the halls, as if we had a shared joke and that joke was the ridiculousness that was Steven. It felt good to have another person to smile at in the hall; with Steven, that made two. I liked it. It wasn't much, but it anchored me. I started looking forward to it. I started preparing funny expressions for when I passed Win. She started making goofy faces at me, too.

It sort of became our thing. Goofy faces, no words.

Steven caught us doing it once.

"You two," he said, and he sounded pleased.

I didn't suspect a thing.

I really didn't suspect a thing.

115

I HAD NO IDEA HOW WRAPPED around the rails Steven was about Noe until one afternoon in art class almost three weeks after he and Noe had broken up. He seemed miraculously intact. Like a friendly universe had granted him a reprieve. I'd seen him campaigning for Pee Sisters in the hall, accompanying this freshman named Kris to the boys' bathroom, playing matchmaker like crazy. It wasn't just me and Win. He spent lunch flitting around the cafeteria, introducing everybody he knew to someone they had to meet. It was like he wanted everyone he cared about to be provided for.

That should have been a sign.

116

IN THE ART MORGUE THAT AFTERNOON, I was feeling better than I had in a long time. Mr. Lim had given my latest self-portrait a pass. Steven had drawn it for me one day at lunch, and it was pretty good.

"What should I call it?" I'd said when he ripped it out of his sketchbook and passed it to me across the table. "*Portrait of the Artist as a Cheater*?"

"The assignment said *any medium*," Steven replied. "In this case, your medium happened to be me."

Steven was wearing a black suit and a black tie. His polished shoes shone under the table. I thought he was dressed that way for something in his drama class. Maybe he was doing a monologue or a one-act play.

"Good morning, Annabeth," he said.

"Good morning, Steven."

"I'd like you to have this," Steven said. He took out the small red mood journal the school counselor was making him carry around.

"Why?" I said.

I noticed he'd drawn a circle around his pinky finger in blue pen. I didn't think anything of it. Steven was always writing stuff on his hands.

"Annabeth Schultz," said Steven. "It's been a pleasure knowing you."

He pushed his chair out from the table and stood up.

"Steven?" I said.

He strode to the long counter where the art supplies were kept. Everyone else had their heads down, working on their paintings. Mr. Lim was marking midterms for his human kinetics class. There was a pleasant hum of industry to the art morgue. Outside the windows, cars were splashing by on the main road. The plastic board outside the Burger King said WHOPPERS 2 X $1.99 CENTS. The funeral parlor still had a Christmas wreath on its front door. I was thinking how sad it was that nobody had taken it down when I heard a *thwack* and Amy McDougall started to scream.

117

HE HAD CUT OFF HIS FINGER. His pinky finger. The one he used to link with Noe's all the time. It shot across the classroom and landed near the recycle bins. If I wasn't sitting right near them, I wouldn't have heard the barely audible tap as it hit the floor.

The art morgue was chaos. Ernestine's ruled cutting surface had blossomed with comically perfect splatters of blood. Steven calmly produced a white handkerchief from his pocket, which he had apparently brought for the purpose, and pressed it to the bleeding stub. Amy McDougall was shrieking.

Mr. Lim shouted at everyone who wasn't Steven to leave the classroom. I pushed toward Steven, but Mr. Lim said, "Out!"

and then the principal and security guard showed up and *they* started hustling everyone out of the classroom, too. On my way out, I ducked and fished Steven's finger out from behind the recycle bins. It had landed in something sticky. I didn't know what to do with it, so I wrapped it in a few tissues from one of the little packets Mom always stuck in my backpack during cold season and put it in my pocket.

In the hall, everyone was milling around like at halftime during a hockey game.

"Shit, did you see that?" people kept saying. Everyone was crowded around the tiny frosted window in the door, trying to see in. You could hear the principal and Mr. Lim's voices, talking to Steven. After a minute, there was an ambulance siren outside. Before I could figure out what to do, Mr. Beek came stomping out of the room.

"Get your butts to the library," he roared.

I hung back. I've never been good at talking to teachers, but with Steven's finger in my pocket I figured it was pretty urgent.

"Library," he barked. "Move it along."

"Excuse me?" I said.

"Move it along, Ms. Schultz," he said. "Steven will be fine."

"Um," I said. "But I need to give his—"

The doors at the end of the hallway burst open and some ambulance people walked in. Mr. Beek clapped his hands.

"Anyone NOT signed in at the library within the next ten

seconds will get to spend their next ten lunch periods in my office."

"I have his finger," I said. "What should I do with it?"

"Go to the library," he said. "Mr. Ternary will give you instructions for the rest of the period."

"No, but—"

I could tell he wasn't listening. But what was I supposed to do? Everything was confusion. Everyone started rushing for the library and somehow I got pulled along. I had a vague idea I would tell the librarian about Steven's finger, but the library was confusion too, with everyone crowding around the table to sign in. I sat in a chair by the newspapers and waited for the line to die down, but I started reading *King Lear*, and the bell was ringing for next period, and I had a midterm in that class and couldn't be late, and somehow I forgot Steven's finger until I was halfway home and put my hands in my pockets to warm them up and felt it there in its bundle of tissue.

I ran the rest of the way home and called Steven's house.

Darla answered the phone.

"It's Annabeth," I said. "I have Steven's finger."

You would be surprised how good some people are at swearing.

118

IT TURNS OUT IT WAS TOO late to save Steven's finger. I guess you're supposed to put it on ice right away. By the time I called Steven's house, the finger was gray and dead and waxy like a candle stub.

To say that it felt weird to have Steven McNeil's dismembered finger in my pocket would be the understatement of the year.

I felt guilty about the finger. I could tell Steven's parents were upset. They tried not to show it, but questions kept popping out.

"You had it in your pocket for how long?" "You went to class with it?" "The principal told you to take it to the *library*?"

Steven's house had stables out back, and a three-car garage. I hadn't realized Steven's family was that rich. I wondered why he went to E. O. James instead of the private school, Forest Oaks, where the kids wear blue blazers with gold buttons up the front and play field hockey instead of normal sports like basketball.

Steven was in his bedroom, which I located only with detailed directions from Darla. When I went in, he was lying on his bed. He wasn't listening to music or anything, just lying there with a scowl on his face, still in his suit, hell, still in his shiny shoes. His right hand was bandaged.

"I'm sorry," I burst out. "I should have taken your finger to the nurse's office."

"Fuck that finger," said Steven. "I never want to see it again."

I sat on the edge of his bed. It had a nice bedspread with matching pillows. It looked like someone other than Steven cleaned his room. There was an acceptance letter from NYU on his desk. I realized that even though he was lying down, Steven's body was rigid, the same as if he were standing. I could feel the tension in his muscles through the mattress. A cat padded into the room, looked around disdainfully, and padded out again.

"She won't even look at me," said Steven.

"I know," I said quietly. "She won't look at me either."

Quiet, quiet. Two rigid people on a bed. I reached over and touched the place where Steven's finger used to be.

119

"**HE'S BETTER OFF WITHOUT HER,**" **WIN** said, shoving an armful of books into her locker. "Steven needs to kiss a few boys before he decides to nest for life with a girl like Noe. Or any girl, really. Or any boy."

"I know," I said. "Once he gets away from his parents, he's going to explode with pent-up brilliance. I wish I was going to be there to see it. I don't think he's even going to realize how badly he was hurting until he goes to New York and experiences something different."

"I think a lot of people are going to realize that once they leave here," Win said.

120

LATER THAT DAY I OVERHEARD NOE conferring with Ms. Bomtrauer by the water fountains. It turned out she was going to assistant coach the E. O. James gym team next year while she was going to Gailer.

Noe stopped carrying around *Foucault's Pendulum*. Now the book under her arm was a catalog of gymnastics equipment. In English she leafed through it with a highlighter, swiping in yellow the item numbers of mats and trampolines and bar equipment. Funding had come through for new leotards: at lunch, the gym birds huddled around a glossy spread of styles to choose from. Did they want a sequined starburst across the breasts, or a sporty flash up each side of the rib cage? I strained my ears to hear Noe's voice in spite of myself, listening to the authoritative way she wielded her new vocabulary of V-necks and bias cuts and sparkle counts.

As I listened to her holding forth on pricing and sizing, a spooky thing danced on the crown of my skull. I thought of her trading air kisses with Darla at the Java Bean and putting girls through their paces at the crumbling YMCA. Buying hair gel at the Walmart, watching circus videos in her bedroom, arranging the dried flowers on her dresser.

Her voice trailed after me all the way out of the cafeteria, like a song you can't get out of your head, a scent you're surprised to find still lingering on your clothes.

You'd be amazed who leaves and who doesn't, at the end of the day.

121

STEVEN WASN'T IN SCHOOL THE NEXT day, or the next. His spot next to mine in the art morgue was empty. The school had run out of art supplies, so we were down to the cheapest possible art form: that old standby, the collage.

I worked on my collage in silence, cutting pictures out of magazines and dutifully gluing them to the page. My collage looked like everyone else's. Maybe the assignment would have worked better if we weren't all cutting things out from the same stack of magazines. Or maybe that was the point: we were all working from the same material, even if we didn't acknowledge it, even if we could trick ourselves into thinking we were so different from one another by holding the scissors differently or getting creative with the layout of the words and images on the page.

Win and I sat together at lunch. Dominic and Kris sat with us too. Sometimes Margot and Eliza joined us and sometimes they didn't. Steven had succeeded in that regard: suddenly, we were our own little friend group. It was actually really nice. If I hadn't been so sad about Steven, it would have been even nicer. I still felt something inside me shrink when I walked past Noe or one of the girls from the gym team, but now at least I had people to be with, and I wasn't completely alone.

"Have you heard anything from Steven?" Win said.

That surprised me. I always assumed everyone was closer with everyone else than I was, but in this case Win thought I was the closer friend, and as I started to talk about Steven I realized it was true.

I am close with Steven, I thought to myself. It was a strange thought. It was strange to think of myself as being close with someone who wasn't Noe. I didn't know it was possible to add people to your repertoire of closeness. I don't know why I thought that; I just did.

"Yeah," I said, and I told Win some of what I knew.

It felt strange to be the person who knew things, instead of the person who had to find them out by asking other people. It meant that someone trusted me. Did that mean that Noe had never trusted me?

I slipped the thought into my pocket with all the others that had been collecting there that year.

122

I WENT TO SEE STEVEN AGAIN later that week. He was still lying on his bed. Still wearing his suit. Still wearing his polished shoes. I wondered if he got dressed like that every morning, or if he had never changed.

"I still have your finger," I said. "It's in my freezer. If you don't ask for it soon, I'm going to get it taxidermied."

When Steven didn't make any sign of answering in the near future, I took out my music player and slipped an earbud into his ear. I lay down beside him on the bed and slipped the other one into my own.

We listened to *The Velvet Underground*, then a few chapters of *Kingdom of Stones*. When I got up to leave, Steven spoke suddenly.

"They all wanted me to cut off a piece of myself."

I paused in his doorway. "Who?"

"Noe. My parents. The school. And I thought, *I'd rather cut off my finger than my soul.*" He looked at me with grim amusement. "I guess that's pretty emo."

I walked back to his bed and sat down. For some reason, my heart had begun to hammer. Normally, I would take that as a sign that I should make a hasty exit or steer the conversation toward a neutral topic, but then a funny thing happened in my throat. An unblocking.

"Steven?" I said. "If I tell you something really personal, will you tell me something really personal?"

"Annabeth Schultz wants to tell me something personal?" Steven said. "Even I'm not messed up enough to skip an opportunity like that."

I HAD THOUGHT THAT THE FIRST time I told anyone about Scott, I would break down. And maybe I would have four years ago. But it was like I'd grown stronger without noticing it, the way a seed doesn't look like much until you turn around and see that it's grown into a tree whose fruit you can actually eat.

"You're the only person I've told," I said to Steven.

He made a small bow. "I'm honored," he said.

There was a beautiful quietness to his bedroom, a sleepiness interrupted only by the occasional noise from downstairs. I thought about how grateful I was for that day in art class when Steven had said, *In that case, we must introduce ourselves.*

How awful it would have been to miss out on all this—to miss out on knowing him. It was no small thing to turn to another human and say, *I want to know you*, with the implied opposite, *I want you to know me*.

"Can I ask you a question?" I said. "What happened the night you tried to kill yourself? With Dominic?"

There was a long silence. Downstairs, I could hear Darla jingling car keys and opening the garage door. When the car had pulled out and the garage door had rumbled closed again, Steven said, "I know what you're really asking."

"You don't have to tell me. It just seems relevant."

A bird called outside Steven's window. He curled his remaining fingers, suddenly agitated.

"The answer is 'I don't know.' It's too loud inside my head to know. When I think about it, all I hear is alarm bells. Nothing happened with Dominic, but he asked very sweetly if I was maybe-possibly-theoretically open to the idea of something happening, and the alarm bells started ringing so loudly it short-circuited my brain. I still don't know if the alarm bells mean I wanted something to happen, or if it was just knowing that I would be completely fucked, in terms of my parents, if I even entertained the possibility. And then I fell in love with Noe and it seemed like everything was going to be okay."

"That's how I felt about Noe, too," I said. "Like she saved me from myself."

"Hear my soul speak," quoted Steven. *"Of the very instant that I saw you, did / my heart fly at your service."*

"I'm glad you're alive," I said, and hugged him.

"I'm glad you're alive, too."

124

DAFFODILS WERE UNFOLDING THEIR YELLOW trumpets in the flower beds in front of my house. At school, we had a motivational speaker come in to talk about the K.E.Y.S. to success. He was thick-necked and greasy and sweated a lot. I sat near the back and read the poem that Loren sent me.

I read while the speaker jabbered and ranted, and while he had the whole auditorium shout the four keys like a cheer, and while the Senior Leaders presented him with a gift bag and shook his hand.

Afterward there was a draw to win a copy of his new book, *The K.E.Y.S. for Students*. I had the winning ticket. I folded it up into an accordion and dropped it on the floor on my way out of the auditorium.

in castles of wind, went the poem. *in halls of rain.*

125

THAT NIGHT I WROTE AN EMAIL to Loren. *I didn't know Wilda McClure wrote poetry.*

He wrote back, *I can send you the book.*

I wrote back, *How was the hike to Garramond Lake?*

By the end of the week, we were emailing two or three times a day.

126

I WENT TO STEVEN'S HOUSE MOST days after school.
He gave me his key so I wouldn't have to talk to Darla when I
came in. She had figured out that I was the girl Noe had told
her about, the one who had refused to die.

"When are you coming back?" I said. "I miss you in Art. My
collage sucks. Win and Dominic miss you, too. Margot Dilforth sends her love."

"I'm not going back," Steven said.

"What do you mean?" I said. "You can't drop out of school.
What about graduation?"

"I'm going to move in with my uncle," he said. "I can finish
my classes online."

"But why?" I sputtered. The thought of finishing the year

without Steven was preposterous. School would be so empty without him. I couldn't imagine graduation without Steven there to make a Royal Society of Pee Sisters salute. "Everyone loves you," I said. "We can figure things out so that you don't ever have to cross paths with Noe and Alex."

"Do you know why I'm lying here?" said Steven.

"Why?"

"It is taking every ounce of effort I have not to kill myself."

"Steven."

"It's okay. I'm not going to do it. I just need to focus."

"Focus on what?"

"Not doing it. And I think that will be a lot easier once I'm living in a place where being myself isn't going to make anyone hate me."

"How will you do it?" I said. "I mean, how is your mom letting you?"

"I'm eighteen," said Steven. "That means nobody has to let you anymore."

"When are you going?"

"Tomorrow. My uncle was all set to come up and get me tonight, but I wanted to say good-bye to you."

"Today's your last day here?"

He nodded. "Hopefully forever."

"In that case," I said. "Let's go. There's something we need to do."

127

WE DROVE TO MY HOUSE TO get the finger out of my
freezer. At my house, I put on Nan's old wedding dress, an armful of beaded necklaces from the Halloween box, and the straw
hat Mom wore to mow the lawn. We made a shrine out of tinfoil and birthday candles and laid the finger inside it. It was
wrinkly at the knuckle and flat and dull at the nail: a stubby
gray saint on its way to a resurrection.

As we drove away from my house, Steven lit the birthday
candles. They cast a warm glow on the finger. Presently the tinfoil was spotted with dots of pink and blue wax.

We went to the Botanical Gardens first to get some flowers for the shrine. It had rained in the morning and now warm

air heaved up from the ground in damp waves. Children in frilly socks were chasing geese across the lawn while their parents strolled along the stone pathways. I led Steven through the labyrinth and past the sundial to the rare plants section to pick some blood lilies and African moonflowers for his finger, but Steven thought they were too pretty to kill so we ended up scooping out handfuls of soil and fertilizer instead, as if Steven's finger were a bulb that could grow a whole new Steven underground.

At the SkyTram I bought him a hot dog. We rode over the river in the shuddering red car. A pair of tourists from Milwaukee asked what happened to Steven's finger. We told them he lost it in the war.

"You look too young to have been in a war," the tourists said, shaking their heads like the world had truly hit the pits. The man of the couple gave Steven a hug and thanked him for his service, and we stood by the gift shop for a long time while they told us about life in Milwaukee.

After the SkyTram we followed the river upstream, parking the car when we got close to the waterfall and going the last half mile on foot. This part of town was always noisy with tour buses and school groups. People were always looking for the bathroom. Still, if you could imagine it without the knick-knack shops and overpriced restaurants, it was an awesome sight.

The waterfall was churning out rainbows. Tourists in gauzy yellow rain ponchos floated along in the mist.

We stood by the railing and said a prayer and threw the finger over. It tumbled down, down, down in its tinfoil coffin like a tiny daredevil in a canoe.

On the way up the walkway, a pair of Australian tourists asked to take our picture. We posed with our arms around each other's shoulders, the waterfall behind us. I think someone said "Cheese" but I couldn't hear it for the roar.

128

A FEW DAYS AFTER STEVEN WENT to New York, I got my first letter from him. It was in a plain white envelope that someone had stepped on; there was a dusty footprint on top of the address.

Dear A, the letter said.

> *How goes the Society of Pee Sisters? Have you gained girth? I miss your furrowed brow. Send me some artwork.*
> *Steven McNeil*

I wrote back:

Dear Steven,

Please find enclosed a Pee Sisters ID card, valid for entry into any opposite-sex bathroom in the Western world. While my brow remains furrowed, the nutritionist assures me I am now eating almost as much as three beavers, six raccoons, or one medium-size deer, which is apparently an improvement. I miss you.

A. Schultz

129

WIN AND I STARTED WRITING OUR one-act play together. We mostly worked at her house. Win had a nice room. We'd get lost in our ideas for hours, thinking up all the details of the set and costumes, writing and rewriting the script. Somehow, bits of other conversations always snuck in.

Win had brown hair that curled on its own. She had a button collection. She was obsessed with anime. She had an older sister who lived in Chicago and was in a band, and a half brother and half sister who lived with their mom in Virginia. She had once spent the night in a cave during a rainstorm. She had a boyfriend, Felix, who was a professional juggler. He was homeschooled, so he could do whatever he wanted, and he traveled around with this juggling troupe and did shows in schools. He had invented a juggling pattern and named it after her: it was called Win's Wiggle and it involved six balls. She showed me a video. It looked hard. The balls went so high, and the flow of them really did seem to wiggle in the air.

One day I was at her house and I noticed a pair of scissors on her desk.

"Hey, Win," I said. "Can you give me a haircut?"

I sat on the floor and she sat above me on her bed. Her hands moved around my head. "How short do you want it?" said Win.

"Short."

"Like bowl-cut short?"

"Like spring chicken short."

"Oh man," giggled Win. She started snipping, *schick, schick, schick*. She snipped forever. Shards of hair fell on my shoulders and lap.

When Win was done cutting my hair, we took a picture of the pile of hair and texted it to Steven. He texted back immediately.

is that what i think it is?

I texted back.

your finger needed company.

I walked home from Win's house feeling lighter. My neck and ears got cold, but it was a good cold, a clean cold.

"You cut your hair!" said Mom. "Wow!"

I smiled back at her, a real smile. I floated wordlessly up the stairs to my room.

130

"NICE HAIRCUT," **SAID BOB.**

"Thanks," I said. "My friend cut it."

When he reached for my food journal, his arm knocked into a stack of basketballs, which promptly collapsed into bouncing, rolling chaos in the tiny office. I leaped up from my chair and Bob leaped up from his. When we had stuffed the basketballs out of the way, we were both disgruntled and Bob was covered in a film of sweat.

"Sorry about that," he said. "They keep saying they'll move those."

"Do you want to get out of here?" I said.

"Where do you want to go?"

"I believe you owe me some pizza," I said.

THE YEAR WAS ROLLING TO AN end. Teachers started opening the windows in classrooms again. Outside the funeral parlor, purple and yellow crocuses were pushing up from the ground. Win and I performed our play at the One-Act Play Festival.

"We dedicate this performance to the memory of Steven McNeil's finger," we announced when we came onstage.

Dominic and Kris filmed it, to send him. The play was surrealist. We wore mustaches, and dug for butterflies that were burrowed underground.

132

IN MAY, JEANETTE FIELDING CALLED TO see if I could pick up a few shifts at the ice-cream shop before coming on full-time in the summer. I had nothing better to do on the weekends, so I said okay.

On my second shift, I was leaning against the counter chatting with Phinnea so I hardly noticed when a family drifted in from the Gardens.

"I'll get this," I said, and I turned to the ice-cream case to take their order.

"Hi there," I said in my usual way. "What can I get for you?"

There were six of them: a mom, a dad, two grandparents, a little girl with pink beads in her hair, and—

Loren Wilder.

Loren Wilder.

Loren Wilder was in the ice-cream shop.

The others were hovering around the ice-cream case, peering down at the flavors. Loren was the tallest, hanging back to let the others see. He saw me too. Our eyes locked, and his face dawned with a smile of surprise.

"Annabeth?" he said.

Phinnea had come up to take the others' orders.

"Hi, Loren," I said.

My body reacted before my brain had a chance to get a word in. I smiled at him, the way water falls, the way rainbows form in the mist. Happiness. It lit inside me, simple as a bird taking off.

"How are you?" he said.

"How are YOU? How was the rock-climbing trip?"

We babbled at each other over the ice-cream case, our words less like words than the spouting of fountains, the happy clanging of trams.

"What kind of ice cream do you want?"

"Um," he said. "Um."

It was as if our smiles had temporarily stunned our brains. Loren widened his eyes and blinked and looked down at the ice cream, but his eyes bubbled back up to me.

"What's good?" he said.

"Pralines and cream," I blurted.

I don't know where it came from. But as soon as I said it, I knew it was true. Pralines and cream was delicious. Pralines and cream was the most exquisite flavor of ice cream in the world. Suddenly, I was filled with the knowledge of sweetness.

"Okay," said Loren. "I'll have that."

We were quiet while I scooped it, although I could tell we were both eager to speak. His grandfather was paying. Phinnea was at the cash register. I handed Loren his cone.

"Do you get off work soon?" said Loren.

"Three o'clock."

"Do you want to—I mean, I could come back," Loren said.

"We can go to the gorge!" I said.

"Yes!" said Loren. "Yes!"

"Loren," shouted his little sister from the door. "We're GOING."

"See you," he said. "I'll come back in—I'll come back."

He hurried out the door after his sister, almost dropping his cone.

I hummed. I buzzed. I felt like a fountain turning on again after a winter spent cradling dry leaves. I bent over the ice-cream case with the scoop.

"Annabeth Schultz," said Phinnea. "Are you making yourself a cone?"

I couldn't speak. I had just taken the first bite.

Portrait of the artist as a person in bliss.

133

THE WEEKEND OF MY GRADUATION, Pauline drove down from Maple Bay. I came home from my last day of school to find her and Mom at the kitchen table with a pot of tea. When I walked in, they looked at me strangely. I said hello, and Pauline gave me a hug.

"How are you, sweetie?" she said.

While she asked me about school, Mom got up from the table and went into the kitchen to refill the teapot. As she walked out, I caught a glimpse of her face. It was filled with an emotion I couldn't name. Something huge. My chest tightened.

Mom stayed in the kitchen for much longer than it takes to fill a kettle with water.

As I chatted with Pauline, I strained my ears for any sound.

I couldn't hear the tap, or the whistle that means boiling. I wondered what Mom was doing. If she was just standing there in the kitchen. If she was frozen by the sink as I'd caught her sometimes, when I was younger, wringing a dishrag as if she was trying to strangle it. Minutes passed and still the kitchen was silent.

Then from the backyard came the sound of chopping wood. I looked Pauline in the eye. "What happened?"

"Scott called."

"What?"

"He wanted to apologize. And ask if he could give her some money. Make some gesture. That sort of thing."

My face went hot. Suddenly, my visit to Baxterville didn't seem so heroic after all. The angry letter he had almost certainly read. I had imagined him begging for forgiveness, but now I wasn't so sure that was a good idea. An apology didn't seem worth the completely intrusive horror of having to hear the sound of his voice on the phone.

"Is she okay?" I said, but before Pauline could answer I was already running outside.

134

MOM WAS BY THE WOODPILE, HER flannel shirt hot
with sweat. When I came outside, she threw down the ax and
gathered me so fiercely into her arms it seemed that both our
bodies would have to break before either of us would let go.

135

ON THE DAY I GRADUATED FROM E. O. James, the scabby black peach trees were covered in a pink snow of blossoms. The puddles at the bottom of our driveway were warm as soup. Mom and Pauline sat in the kitchen talking while I brushed my hair and brushed my teeth and wriggled my feet into the dress shoes that Nan had taken me to buy at the mall the day before.

Graduation was a joke. Mr. Beek gave a funny speech that mentioned each graduate by name, even the ones he had never actually talked to in the four years we were here. They flashed our freshman-year photos on a projector screen. Mine showed a wide-eyed girl in glasses. Noe's showed a baby-faced kid in a Winnie the Pooh sweater. Over the past few months, our friendship had become a mystery to me, but when I looked at those pictures, I remembered who I had been when I needed Noe the most, and who she had been when she needed me. Maybe none of us can tell what we're becoming until we become it, like seedlings instinctively groping for certain nutrients without knowing why.

After the graduation ceremony, everyone spilled outside, where next year's Senior Leaders had set up refreshment tables with cake and coffee and sparkling apple juice. From the place where I was standing with Mom and Pauline and Ava and my uncle Dylan, I saw Noe turning a cartwheel on the grass, keys falling out of her pockets as her legs arced through the sky.

Something in my heart broke, then. I put down my cake plate and ran to her. We didn't talk, but turned cartwheels on the soccer field, mortarboards falling off, hands staining green from the grass.

When I thought of the girl in my freshman-year picture, I couldn't imagine her leaving Noe to do it alone.

136

MOM ASKED ME WHAT I WANTED for a graduation present. "It can't be too extravagant," she added, as if I would ever dream of asking for something like a new car or a new computer or a trip to Mexico.

"I want you to take me canoeing," I said.

137

WE DROVE UP TOGETHER THE WEEK before the fall
semester started. We packed matches and knives, string and
sunscreen, oats and coffee. Uncle Dylan dug Mom's old canoe
out from the back of his garage and we spent a weekend rub-
bing the paddles with linseed oil and patching a small leak in
the stern. On the drive up, the tip of the canoe poked out over
the front of the truck, pointing like an arrow toward the north.
Trees rippled on either side of the road, lush and green in their
summer fullness.

When we put into the water at Maple Bay, the canoe leaped
forward with a speed and power that astounded me. Soon the
docks melted away behind us, and the families paddling around

the bay in their bright yellow rental canoes, and we entered a silence unlike any I'd experienced before. In the silence was a whirring warbling dripping of paddles, musical greens and blues. I was almost afraid to look behind me in case Mom had vanished, in case the woods had reabsorbed her, greedily embraced her in their twigs and mosses.

I wondered if I would always feel her that way, as a strength propelling me, a guiding silence in my canoe. I saw them, then, the ghosts quietly slipping out from under us. I could feel mine leave me, a weightlessness. I cut my paddle into the water and felt the wilderness rush toward me, and the wilderness inside me tremble and flower, rushing, rushing toward it.

Don't miss these titles by
Hilary T. Smith